Shooting STARS

PAUL BUCHANAN & ROD RANDALL

CPH
SAINT LOUIS

The Misadventures of Willie Plummet

Invasion from Planet X
Submarine Sandwiched
Anything You Can Do I Can Do Better
Ballistic Bugs
Battle of the Bands
Gold Flakes for Breakfast
Tidal Wave
Shooting Stars
Hail to the Chump
The Monopoly

Cover illustration by John Ward.
Back cover photo by Ira Lippke.
Cover and interior design by Karol Bergdolt.

Copyright © 1998 Rod Randall
Published by Concordia Publishing House
3558 S. Jefferson Avenue, St. Louis, MO 63118-3968

Manufactured in the United States of America

Library of Congress Cataloging-in-Publication Data

Buchanan, Paul, 1959-
      Shooting Stars / Paul Buchanan & Rod Randall.
      p.   cm. — (The misadventures of Willie Plummet)
      Summary: When thirteen-year-old Willie applies for a job as a stuntman on a movie set, he finds himself following a series of wrong paths which get him into a succession of misadventures.
      ISBN 0-570-05087-1
      [1. Motion pictures—Production and direction—Fiction.   2. Stunt performers—Fiction. 3. Conduct of life—Fiction.]   I. Randall, Rod, 1962-   . II. Title.   III. Series: Buchanan, Paul, 1959-   Misadventures of Willie Plummet.
PZ7.B87717Sh   1998
[Fic]—dc21
                                                                                                              98-7205
                                                                                                              AC

1   2   3   4   5   6   7   8   9   10   07   06   05   04   03   02   01   00   99   98

For Lauryn

Contents

① Revenge of the Raven

I ducked just before the giant raven took off my head. It cast a shadow the size of a plane and squawked like some kind of prehistoric bird.

"That was close," Felix's voice cracked. As one of my best friends, he had the misfortune of being nearby whenever one of my adventures went sour.

"Tell me about it," I whispered. "Those claws almost scalped me. But I wasn't afraid or anything."

Sam offered a doubtful glance. Her real name is Samantha, and as another one of my close friends, she knew me too well. "Sure, Willie. That's why your arms are covered with goose bumps."

"I'm just cold," I said, rubbing my arms.

As the dark beast soared into the clouds, we all straightened up. When the raven reappeared, it dropped like a heat-seeking missile. Its talons moved into position.

"Hit the dirt!" Felix shouted, diving for the ground. His voice sounded like a drill sergeant's.

The raven swooped within inches of our heads before spiraling into the sky. As we rose to our feet, I noticed one of the assistant directors glaring at us. He brought his index finger to his lips.

"Felix," I whispered. "We're supposed to be quiet. Remember?"

"I know," Felix said, getting defensive. "But I can't control my voice. I think it's changing."

Sam watched the scene with a look of wonder on her face. "This is so awesome."

I felt the same way—and not just about the raven. I was blown away by the whole production: the sets, props, lighting—you name it. I couldn't believe an actual movie crew had come to Glenfield.

The director sat in a folding wooden chair, eyeing everything with the intensity of a surgeon. He wore a green ball cap that struggled to contain his bushy gray hair. The tails of his yellow flannel shirt hung casually untucked over slightly faded jeans.

Customized trailers were parked along the street for the movie's stars and important crew members. A catering tent provided endless refreshments. Cables stretched in every direction, running power to lights and cameras. There was even a generator truck on-site—called the "Grip and Electric"—that cranked out the needed amps to keep everything operating.

Now only one challenge remained: I, Willie Plummet, needed to land a part in the movie. Action scenes would be my specialty. I'd jump from buildings, fall out of planes, and dodge bullets. I'd travel the world, going from one daring feat to the next. And it would all begin right here with *Revenge of the Raven*, the movie they had come to shoot in my own backyard. Well, not literally *my* backyard, but close enough.

The actual location was the Pike Estate, Glenfield's only national historic landmark. Colonel Pike had rented the whole place to the production company. With a three-story house and expansive grounds that included a barn, corral, and adjoining field, his estate was the perfect place to film a movie.

Felix, Sam, and I knew the estate like we knew our own backyards. After all, we had helped Colonel Pike save his property from road construction—and robbery. But that's another story.

"Willie, look out," Sam muttered. She jerked me down just as the raven swooped by.

"Where's your head?" Felix asked. "In the stars ?"

"I can't help it," I whispered. "All I can think about is getting a part in the movie."

Felix wiped the dust from his glasses with the back of his sleeve. "You? An actor?"

I shook my head. "Not an actor, a stuntman. I could do all the fun stuff without having to learn lines."

"Well, if things work out and you need an agent, let me know," Felix said.

"Thanks, but no thanks," I said.

"Too bad for you Trenton Kyle does all his own stunts," Sam told me, keeping her voice low. "Not that it's hard to see why. Look at him. What a hunk."

Trenton Kyle crouched in worn boots, jeans, and a white T-shirt. He had blue eyes, muscular arms, and iron abs. His coarse brown hair fell across his forehead. In this scene, he was protecting his little sister from the giant raven's deadly claws.

"Quick, we've got to reach the barn!" Trenton Kyle urged the girl who was playing his young sibling.

"But I'm afraid," the starlet cried out.

"Don't be," Trenton said. "I've got bravery enough for two."

"Oh, gag me," I moaned. "Another line like that and I'll have barf enough for two."

"Shhh!" Sam hushed, a dreamy haze in her eyes.

"And you guys accuse me of getting lost in the stars," I protested. "Sam, you should see yourself."

"Shhh!" she said again. She pulled her blonde hair behind her ears to make sure nothing obstructed her view of the Hollywood hunk.

Trenton scooped his little sister into his bulging arms and raced for the barn. The raven zeroed in like a feathered torpedo.

"*Caw! Caw!*" the black beast cried, full of rage.

"Hurry!" the little sister begged.

We watched the robotic raven, with a wing span of 15 feet, drop straight for Trenton and the starlet.

How would they dodge it this time? I wondered.

Whamo! That answered that question. They wouldn't. The raven smashed into Trenton Kyle's back and knocked him to the ground. The starlet flew from his arms and sailed into the corral. The raven followed suit, hitting the dirt beside her with a thud.

"Cut!" the director yelled. He ran straight for Trenton Kyle.

"Ouch! My ankle!" the girl cried.

Seeing that Trenton Kyle was okay, the director turned his attention to the actress. Soon she was surrounded by the crew. Everyone was talking at once, including the Glenfield residents who had gathered to watch the filming from behind the barricades.

Leonard "the Crusher" Grubb, a fellow junior high student with a high tolerance for pain—especially when he was inflicting it on someone else—balked at the whole thing. "She ain't hurt. It's all special effects," he said.

"What are you talking about?" I challenged. "The director yelled '*Cut!*' and she's still screaming."

Crusher stepped toward me. "Are you calling me a liar, Plummet?"

Before I could answer, the starlet let out another cry, still wincing in agony. It wasn't long before a guy with the crew came over and whispered something to the security guard. The guard in turn dismissed us all. "That's a wrap for today, folks."

Reluctantly, everyone began to leave the Pike Estate. The young actress continued to moan as more crew members came and went.

"You guys can leave if you want to," I said. "I'm going to find the director. After that accident, he may insist on hiring a stuntman for Trenton Kyle."

"Willie, from this side of the barricade, you can't even talk to the director," Sam reminded me. "How do you expect to get a part?"

"Follow me," I said. I led the way across the estate of our good friend Colonel Pike. Walking along the side of the house, we reached a small gate that led into the backyard. "Here we are. Remember that Bible verse that talks about taking the small gate? What more could you ask for?"

"Isn't that verse about following the Lord instead of the world?" Sam asked.

"That's what I thought," Felix agreed. "As I remember it, the small gate is contrasted with a wide gate. Lots of people take the wide gate because it's easy. But in the end, they pay for it."

"I know that," I said defensively. "But who says God doesn't want us to get involved in the movie? This gate can be sort of a symbolic step."

"Are you serious?" Sam asked, exchanging a look with Felix.

"Sure. Hold me to it," I replied, then led them through the gate into the backyard.

Once inside Colonel Pike's backyard, Felix turned his attention to the giant raven still lodged in the dirt. "Sam, keep an eye on Willie. I think I'll have a talk with the guy in charge of special effects."

As Felix wandered off, Sam and I watched the young actress as she was carried to a car. I felt sorry for her and hoped her injury wasn't too serious. From the grimace on her face and the way she held her foot, it didn't look good.

Once the car drove away, the director talked to his assistants. Every time one walked away, another would appear with what seemed to be urgent news.

"Well, Sam, here goes nothing," I said, walking toward the director.

At first he didn't notice me. But after clearing my throat a few times, one of the assistants stepped aside.

"Excuse me, sir," I started off, trying to sound confident. "My name is Willie Plummet. I'd like to apply for a job as a stuntman."

The director's eyes traveled from me to his assistants, then back to me again. I couldn't tell if he was annoyed or impressed. But at least I had his attention.

"A stuntman, huh?" he replied.

I nodded and listed some of my experiences. "Once, I out-ran a poacher at Pinnacle Lake. Another time, I barely escaped a swarm of bees. I even helped discover a secret tunnel beneath the ground we're standing on."

When I finished, one of the director's assistants whispered something into his ear. The director listened intently to his assistant's suggestion, then turned his attention to me. "Sounds like you're the kind of guy who gets the job done."

"You bet," I answered.

"You're not afraid to get your hands dirty?" the director asked.

"No way. My hands are always dirty. Filthy. Disgusting. Covered with grime," I replied.

"Perfect," the director said and grinned. He grabbed one of the men standing nearby. "I'd like you to meet Robert Karpman, our location manager. He's got just the job for you. Welcome to show business."

As the location manager led me away, I grinned like a chimpanzee. My first big break and all I'd had to do was ask. Sam remained behind, standing awkwardly near the director and his assistants. I could see the longing in her eyes and couldn't blame her. She was still a normal eighth-grader, and I was on my way to the top.

Behind the barn the location manager stopped and faced me. He had short dark hair and wore tan leather boots. "Willie, welcome to the crew of *Revenge of the Raven*. Glad to have you aboard. You can call me Rob."

"Good to meet you, Rob," I said, shaking his hand.

"You've already seen the large mechanical raven, but what you haven't seen is the real ones that appear in the beginning of the film. Say hello to Liz and Biz." Rob uncovered a large cage containing two ravens. They had sharp beaks and claws and the shiniest black feathers I'd ever seen.

"*Caw! Caw!*" they both sounded off. "*Caw! Caw!*"

"Which is which?" I asked.

"Liz is the smaller one. She has the silver band around one of her legs." The ravens looked me over, then pecked at the wire mesh.

"So what's this movie all about, anyway?" I asked.

Rob gave me a quick overview of the plot—one of those typical action/horror stories. "Basically, the entire movie revolves around these two birds," he finished.

I listened intently while stepping closer to the ravens' cage. Too close. One whiff of the foul odor and I wanted to gag. I waved my hand in front of my nose. "In that case, someone should clean their cage."

"Bingo," Rob said, slapping me on the back. "That's where you come in."

"What?" I choked. "What happened to '*Welcome to show business*'?"

"We all have to start somewhere. Besides, when it comes to a successful picture, everyone's role is critical, whether you're the big-time stuntman or the peon birdcage cleaner."

"Thanks for the pep talk," I said, holding my nose. "But if you don't mind, I'll take big-time stuntman any day."

Rob shrugged. "You never know, champ. If you handle this job well, you may get your wish. Anyway, do your best and make sure you get the corners. If the wire brush won't reach, you have my permission to use your fingernails."

I was too stunned to respond with even one wisecrack.

"Use the small side door to clean the cage," Rob continued. "If you use the large one on top, the birds might get out. Be careful with them or we'll both be out of work." With that he took off to check on something else.

This could only happen to me, I thought. Instead of starring, getting my big break, I'm stuck cleaning up after a couple of ravens. This gave a whole new meaning to the phrase, "There's no business like show business."

"*Caw! Caw!*" Liz called out.

"I'll take that as a *thank you*," I said. Biz stretched his wings, then pecked at one of the droppings.

"Okay. Okay. I'll get started." Easing toward the cage, I opened the latch. Suddenly, Liz and Biz grew silent and suspiciously still. Their black eyes followed my every move, as if stalking their prey.

Grabbing the wire brush, I put my hand inside the ravens' cage and started scraping.

Biz looked especially hungry. He licked his beak. He eyed my hand like it was a pork chop. Good thing there wasn't a packet of ketchup in his claw.

"Whew!" I gasped. "No offense, but you guys are pigs. For a couple of Hollywood ravens, your grooming habits are terrible."

I scraped at the bottom of the cage, but the dry droppings would hardly budge. Working through the small door didn't help. I could barely move my arm. Before long the ravens got bored with me. They settled in the back of the cage and closed their eyes. I felt like doing the same thing. At the rate I was going, it would be days before I finished.

Then I realized something. With the ravens asleep, I could work through the big door on top of the cage. Sleeping birds don't fly away. And I'd get better leverage with the brush.

I closed the small door, then carefully twisted the latch on top. Liz and Biz didn't stir. Moving slowly, I raised the wide door until it was open all the way. The ravens remained quiet and motionless. Grabbing the wire brush, I carefully lowered my hand inside the open cage. Easy. Quiet. Steady as she goes.

"Dude! What's up?" Felix boomed as he approached.

The brush jerked forward and rattled the cage. Biz jumped like he had been goosed, then pecked my hand.

"Ouch!" I hollered, stepping away.

Biz sensed the opportunity and took flight through the top of the cage.

"Get back," I ordered.

"*Caw! Caw!*" Biz replied, flapping his wings and flying toward freedom.

"No!" I gasped. Jumping forward, I locked the cage before Liz could escape too. But Biz was long gone. The last I saw of him, he was heading over the barn and into the clouds.

"Just between me and you," I said to Liz, "this can't be good."

Liz scratched at one of the droppings in the cage as if to say, "You missed a spot."

When Felix came over, I let him have it. "What's with the loud mouth?"

"I told you my voice is changing," he explained, a little taken aback by my anger. "What's going on, anyway?"

"Later," I said, knowing I had to go after Biz. But before I could, Rob returned.

"Where's Biz?" he demanded, staring at the cage.

"He sort of, like, went out for some fresh air. I'm sure he'll be right back," I said.

"You let him out?" Rob hollered. Dust clouded under his boots as he stomped back and forth, searching the sky. "Don't tell me you used the top door."

"It was an accident," I said. "I'm really sorry. If it wasn't for—"

"Wait until the wrangler arrives," Rob fumed.

"The wrangler?" I asked.

"That's what they call the person in charge of the animals in a movie," Rob explained. "Right now our wrangler is finishing up on another production. But he's due here any day. Liz and Biz are his star pets."

I glared at Felix, but he didn't let out a peep. Sure, *now* he was quiet.

Rob put his hand on my shoulder. "Listen—we're not scheduled to use the ravens for two days. I hope the wrangler won't arrive before then. That gives you 48 hours to find Biz. Got it?"

I swallowed hard. "At the rate he was flying, he's probably in another state by now."

Rob shook his head. "Liz and Biz aren't just mates in the movie, they're mates in real life. As long as Liz is here, Biz won't go far. Now get out there and catch him!"

I took off fast, searching the sky as I ran. But with my head in the clouds, it was hard to see where I was going. I had no sooner passed the corral than I tripped over a power cable—which, unfortunately, was attached to a camera. As the huge tripod crashed to the ground, I tumbled into the director's chair, taking him to the ground with me. By the time we stopped rolling, we looked like two finalists in a human knot contest.

"It's like I was saying," I informed the director, trying to make the best of it. "If things get too dangerous for Trenton Kyle, I'm something of a stuntman."

"Oh, you're something, all right." The director climbed to his feet and brushed himself off. "You, Plummet, are definitely something."

I decided not to bring up the little mishap with the ravens and took off again, making my way through the streets of Glenfield. This time I kept one eye on the sky and the other on earth. I searched trees, high wires, and every rooftop in sight. But Biz, the Hollywood raven, was nowhere to be found.

That night I sat in our family room, an encyclopedia lying open in front of me. I figured that if I was going to find Biz, I needed to learn everything I could about ravens.

Mom and my older sister, Amanda, sat at a table working on ceramics. Glenfield had scheduled a big craft fair in a week. Mom and Amanda planned to set up a booth to sell their work.

Dad and Orville were watching a special on military aircraft. Dad recently had built a working model of the Stealth bomber. He wanted to see how the model compared to the real thing.

"I still can't believe you lost one of the ravens," Orville said during a commercial.

"You should have seen the chunk of skin he took out of my finger," I said, displaying the red mark for everyone to see.

"I've seen pimples bigger than that," Orville replied.

"Let's keep your face out of this," I said. "The point is, Biz had a plan. He's one smart bird, which is exactly what the encyclopedia says about ravens. Then again, Biz would have to be a genius to outsmart Willie Plummet."

I waited for, "You got that right!" or "That's for sure!" But Mom and Dad were silent. Amanda just rolled her eyes at Orville.

"So what's the movie called again?" Dad asked.

"*Revenge of the Raven*," I told him.

"Sounds like a real winner," Orville said.

I offered a brief explanation of the plot. "It's about a small town that's terrorized by a mutant, revenge-seeking raven—hence the name, *Revenge of the Raven*. The story begins with an evil town council that decides to cut down a giant oak tree in a vacant field. The council claims it's a fire hazard, but the members really want the wood for furniture."

"Furniture, huh?" Dad noted, obviously intrigued.

"Exactly," I said. "The council knows that a pair of ravens is nesting in the tree, but they chainsaw the towering oak to smithereens."

"Do the birds die?" Amanda asked.

"Only the female," I clarified. "The male flies away. He ends up nesting in a barn that happens to be jam-packed with growth hormones used on cattle."

"A regular growth-hormone hideout," Orville chimed in.

"Exactly. The people of the town think the raven is gone for good," I continued. "But they're wrong. He comes back in a *big* way, with a vengeance."

"I'll tell you one thing I like—the film's title," Dad said. "There's incredible potential for sequels. For instance, *Return of the Raven* has a nice ring to it."

"Or *Remorse of the Raven*," Orville added. "It could be about a kinder, gentler raven that feels guilty for pecking everyone's eyes out."

"What about *Re-cast of the Raven*?" Amanda suggested. "Instead of a raven, the movie could star a 13-year-old redhead in a pigeon suit."

"Oh, that's real funny," I said, getting annoyed.

Unfortunately, everyone else in the family was in hysterics. They suggested one title after another, laughing all the time.

To tune them out, I studied the encyclopedia, hungry for more information. It mentioned the raven's wingspan—up to 30 inches; its range—nearly half of the United States; and its diet—insects, small rodents, and produce.

"That's it!" I announced. "I can lure Biz back with bait. It will be just like catching fish in Lunker Lake."

"It's worth a try," Dad said, returning his attention to the Stealth bomber on TV.

The key would be picking the right bait. The encyclopedia mentioned produce. I could slice up some fresh vegetables. But Glenfield was full of gardens. Why would Biz seek out my plate of tomatoes and zucchini? I needed something more tempting. Something a raven couldn't resist.

"How's that look?" Amanda held up her latest ceramic creation for Mom to see. It was a mouse.

"Beautiful," Mom said.

I couldn't have agreed more. Except for the little red vest, Amanda's mouse looked like the real thing.

"See how hard work pays off?" Mom said. "That little guy will be the talk of the craft fair."

"Like it?" Amanda asked, noticing my stare.

I nodded. My mind was spinning. It could work. It had to work. Tomorrow I'd heist the ceramic mouse—I mean *borrow* it—then find the perfect location to set my trap. With a little help from Felix and Sam, we'd catch Biz. Mr. Hollywood Raven would be back in his cage with 24 hours to spare.

⌇⌇⌇

I decided the best place to catch Biz would be in the oak tree at the Pike Estate. The location was close to Liz and offered plenty of thick foliage to conceal Felix and the net I'd brought along.

"You're sure this will work?" Felix squeaked nervously. He walked with me toward the base of the tree. "It's an awfully small net."

"Sure. It's perfect," I replied.

Felix held up the backpacking hammock I'd brought from home, as if to give me a chance to reconsider. The hammock was made of nylon net and measured about six-feet square.

I grabbed one end of the hammock and showed Felix what to do. "As long as you drop the net directly over Biz as he grabs the mouse, we'll be okay."

"Why do *I* have to drop the net?" Felix asked.

"Because I have to jump out and grab Biz when the net lands on him. You can do it if you want, but that bird is already a proven man-eater." I showed Felix my cut from the day before.

"Are you sure that's not a mosquito bite?" Felix asked.

"Yes. And it's not a pimple either."

Reaching into my pocket, I took out the ceramic mouse and placed it a short distance from the trunk of the oak tree.

"That mouse looks just like the real thing!" Felix exclaimed. "Except, of course, for the red vest. I can't believe Amanda let you use it."

"Well, she didn't actually *let* me," I clarified. "But as long as I return it unharmed before she realizes it's gone, I have nothing to worry about. What Amanda doesn't know won't hurt her."

"So in other words, you stole it," Felix observed.

"I didn't steal it. I borrowed it. There's a differ-ence," I answered.

Felix just looked at me, unconvinced. "What about this hammock? It's not yours either, is it?"

"No. It's Orville's," I explained, starting to get defensive. "I borrowed it too."

"Or so you think," Felix blurted out, his voice sud-denly deep and suspicious. "What happened to yes-terday's small gate? Remember? Following the Lord's way instead of the world's?"

"Keep it down or you'll scare Biz away for good," I said, trying to change the subject. I felt a twinge of guilt. I should have asked for permission, but I could-n't think about that right now, not with Biz on the loose. "Come on, Felix. Hurry and climb the tree."

Felix reluctantly positioned himself on a limb directly above the ceramic mouse.

After donning a pair of thick leather gloves, I crawled under a nearby bush. I checked my watch, thinking it could be awhile before Biz appeared.

Boy, was I wrong. In less than 10 minutes, the bird arrived. At first he circled high above us. Then he gradually spiraled lower. I looked up at Felix to make sure he was ready. He still held the net, but his atten-tion was directed toward the Pike Estate. I had no idea what he was looking at and I didn't care. My con-cern was 100 percent Biz.

"Felix," I whispered, desperate to get his attention. He didn't hear me.

Meanwhile, Biz swooped to within a few feet of the mouse.

"Felix! Net!" I hissed. Again, no response.

Biz angled around and dove for the ceramic mouse. In one fluid motion he extended his claws and swept up his prey. Felix stared at the Pike Estate, totally unaware of what was happening beneath him.

With a few flaps of his wings, Biz flew beyond the shadow of the oak tree. I didn't know if I should bury my face in the dirt or climb the tree and knock Felix out of it. I was furious. Not only had we missed a perfect chance to catch Biz, but Amanda's prize ceramic mouse was gone.

I watched in horror, certain that once Biz realized his catch was fake, he would drop it from a hundred yards up. Amanda's mouse would shatter like glass, just like my eardrums would when she started screaming at me. But an amazing thing happened. Biz glided into a U-turn and landed in the exact spot where he had picked up the mouse.

I glanced at Felix, hoping he had noticed. But he was still in a trance, staring at the Pike Estate.

Still holding the mouse, Biz gave it a light peck, then stared at it. I couldn't wait any longer. I had to do something. Hidden by the bush, I moved into a crouch, ready to pounce.

My timing couldn't have been better. Biz noticed something in the direction of the Pike Estate and turned his back to me. That was all I needed.

Ready. Set. Go!

I leapt from the bush and extended my hands. It was like trying to catch a pass in the end zone. Just before I made the grab, though, Biz hopped out of my reach, taking the ceramic mouse with him.

"Come back!" I yelled, lying spread-eagle on the ground.

My voice must have startled Felix because the next thing I knew, the nylon hammock dropped over my head. I scrambled up, trying to throw it off so I could make another grab for Biz. But I tripped and fell face-first in the dirt.

"*Caw! Caw!*" Biz chuckled, then took off again.

Climbing down from his perch, Felix gave me a curious look. "Was I too slow on the drop?"

"Just a tad," I muttered.

"Sorry, but when I saw the location manager get out the mechanical raven, I got distracted," Felix said.

Biz could have perched on your head and you wouldn't have noticed," I replied.

"Speaking of Biz, at least he's still around." Felix pointed to the top of the oak tree. Biz was resting on a branch, holding the ceramic mouse.

"You wait here," I told Felix. "With a good toss of this hammock, that bird is mine."

After tying the hammock around my waist, I quickly worked my way up the tree. As if to make my job easier, Biz dropped down a little and perched on the end of a thick branch that was practically horizontal to the ground. It was also free of little twigs and leaves that might catch in the net.

Edging along the branch, I stopped within throwing range and untied the hammock. Biz glanced in my direction, then returned his attention to the mouse. With a good toss, I could cover Biz with the net. I dangled the hammock below me, ready to let it fly.

"Willie?" a broken voice called. It was Felix.

"Not now," I muttered through tight lips.

"Willie?" the voice whispered.

"Later," I said, fearful that Biz would split.

He did. And a moment later I found out why. I turned just as the giant raven swooped straight for me. I couldn't react in time. It hit me like a meteor, knocking me from the branch. I landed on my back with a thud. The hammock followed, covering me from head to toe.

"That hammock has your name on it," Felix said, dividing his attention between me and the mechanical raven.

"Why didn't you warn me?" I grumbled.

"I tried."

"You whispered!" I told him. "That's not trying. You should have yelled your head off! Something like: Willie! Duck or die!"

Felix complained, "One minute my voice is too loud; the next it's too quiet. I can't win."

I was too frustrated to get up, so I just stayed on the ground, searching the sky for Biz. But he had disappeared. The giant raven had scared him away during its ballistic assault on the tree.

"I think you damaged the robotic raven when it knocked you out of the tree," Felix said.

"What do you mean, *I* damaged the raven?" I asked.

We watched the giant raven wobble through a turn, then lose altitude. Halfway back to the barn, the raven crashed to the ground. Rob ran to it immediately. Felix and I met him there.

"Bad week for ravens," I said as I walked up.

"Tell me about it," Rob said. He realigned the tail feathers, then turned his attention to one of the wings. "Any sign of Biz?"

"I almost had him. But he got away when your robotic raven knocked me out of the oak tree."

"That's bad news," Rob said. "With this thing still under repair, the director might want to shoot a few scenes with Liz and Biz before the wrangler arrives. There's no other option, unless the new actress who plays Trenton Kyle's younger sister can learn some lines by this afternoon."

"New actress? Who?" I asked.

"I can't remember," Rob said with a shrug. "I know she's from around here. And as I recall, she had a weird name for a girl."

I looked at Felix. From his expression, I knew he was thinking the same thing I was.

"The girl's name wasn't *Sam*, was it?" I asked.

"Yeah, I think so. What's that short for—Samuel?" Rob asked, obviously a little too focused on the mechanical bird.

I elbowed Felix. "Yeah, that's right."

"Don't listen to him, " Felix said. He knelt next to Rob and the giant raven. "Sam is short for Samantha."

I glanced toward the Pike Estate, wondering if Sam was there now. She hadn't been at home when I'd called that morning. I'd wanted her to help catch Biz, and considering how things had gone, we could have used her. But had she really landed a part in the movie? I decided to check it out for myself.

After a short walk, I reached the barn where the crew had filmed the day before. Other than a few crew members milling about, the place looked deserted. No wonder Rob was so uptight. Nothing was getting done.

"Excuse me. Have you seen a girl by the name of Sam?" I asked one of the crew members.

"I think her trailer is over there," he said, pointing to the street.

Her trailer? I nearly gagged. Sam had gotten a part in the movie *and* her own trailer? It had to be a mistake.

It wasn't. At the end of a string of trailers, each marked with an important title or name, was Samantha Stewart's trailer. I stared at the gold letters for a while, then got up the nerve to knock.

After a few moments, Sam opened the door. She greeted me with, "Willie, darling, how good of you to stop by. Won't you come in?"

My mouth dropped open. "Sam, tell me I'm dreaming."

"Actually, I'm the one living a dream," she said with a smile.

When I stepped inside her trailer, I could see why. It had plush carpet and comfortable furniture. A bouquet of flowers and a box of chocolates rested on the coffee table. Cans of soda and fancy mineral waters filled the refrigerator. More *hors d'oeuvres* than I'd known existed covered the counter.

"Mind if I help myself?" I asked. Before Sam could answer, I spread some cheese on a cracker and popped it into my mouth.

"Willie, you silly boy, that was makeup," Sam said, pointing at the tin I had eaten from.

"Yuck!" I gagged, spitting the paste across the trailer. After taking a drink of soda, I turned to Sam. "So why didn't you call me with the big news?"

"It all happened so fast," Sam said. "When the actress got hurt yesterday, I stayed to talk with the director. My experience as a television intern must have impressed him. When he found out that she'd broken her foot and would be out for six weeks, he gave me a call."

"I don't believe it."

"Tell me about it. My parents were here all morning, talking to the director and signing the contract. Now everything's official. Come on, let me show you around." Sam grabbed my hand and led me outside.

As Sam pulled me along she described what the different trucks and trailers were for. "That's craft services. They make sure that snacks and drinks are always available for the crew. That's the property truck. The mechanical raven and other props are stored there. Over there's the honeywagon. That has the restrooms in it."

"Nice name," I said, rolling my eyes. As we walked along, Sam pointed out everything else she had learned about the movie lot.

"What can I say, Sam? I'm impressed."

Sam smiled, but she quickly tried to downplay the significance of her part. "I don't have that many lines."

Hearing her mention *lines* reminded me why I'd come over. "Since you don't have that many, could you learn them by the end of the day?"

"Today? The director said I have three days," Sam said, her eyes wide in terror.

"Well, there may be a change of plans."

"How do you know? Did you get hired as a stunt-man?" Sam asked.

"Not exactly, but I am part of the crew," I replied.

"Really? Doing what?" Sam asked.

"Cleaning the birdcage."

Sam laughed, then forced herself to stop. "Well, that's a start. I mean, at least your foot's in the door, which is better than in your mouth."

"You celebrities sure do have a way with words," I replied dryly. "If things don't change soon, I won't have a foot anywhere near this picture." I told Sam everything that had happened with Biz and Amanda's prize mouse. "The worst part was getting knocked from the tree by that mechanical raven."

"I was wondering what happened to you," Sam said. "You look like you tried to beat up the ground with your face."

"Thanks, that's just how I feel." I glanced up in the sky, taking a quick look for Biz. All I found was blue. "Just promise me you'll learn your lines as quickly as possible."

"I'll try," Sam said, tucking her blonde hair behind her ears. "But no promises."

Frustrated, I walked Sam back to her trailer. "Come on, Sam. Promise me you won't leave this trailer until you know your lines."

"Don't sweat it, W. P. I'll work with you." With that, Sam stepped inside her trailer and closed the door in my face.

Crossing the production area, I headed to where I had left Felix and Rob. Sam sounded a little too iffy, even for an actress. I would have felt a lot better if the mechanical raven were flying again. Otherwise the director would come looking for Liz and Biz and I'd be off the set for good.

When I rounded the barn, I saw Felix. He was alone, standing over the mechanical raven.

"Where's Rob?" I asked.

"Gone. The director decided to shoot a scene with Trenton Kyle inside the Pike house. Rob needed to help with the props," Felix explained.

"Cool," I said. "The director came up with something that doesn't require Biz. That should buy me a little time."

"You mean *us*. Guess who's the new props assistant for *Revenge of the Raven*."

"I don't believe it."

"Believe it," Felix squeaked with enthusiasm. "When I told Rob about the lab in the storeroom of your dad's shop and about all of our experience with model planes and rockets, he hired me to fix the raven."

"Why just you?"

"I guess after you let Biz get loose, he wasn't ready to give you more responsibility. Not after you messed up so royally on such a simple task."

"But you're the one who woke up Biz with your big mouth," I reminded him.

"I guess I forgot to mention that to Rob."

"This is unbelievable," I said. "Sam is in the movie. You're the props assistant. All I am is the soon-to-be-fired birdcage cleaner."

"Don't sweat it, Willie. As long as you don't tell Rob, I'll let you be my unofficial helper." Felix leaned over and picked up the mechanical bird. When he did, an updraft caught the long black wings. As the raven lifted overhead, Felix clung to its legs, trying to keep his feet on the ground.

For a moment I thought it would be fun to let the robotic raven drag Felix across the field. Then I remembered the small gate and figured if I didn't help him, I'd regret it. Grabbing the raven, I held on tightly while Felix folded the giant wings against the bird's body. After that we headed for the lab.

In the storeroom of Plummet's Hobbies, we cleared a space on the floor and got to work on the raven. The first thing we needed to do was install gears with finer teeth. Then the wing adjustments could be more precise.

"Now to deal with the uplift problem," Felix said.

"What do you mean?" I asked. "This thing lifted you without a problem, or it was about to."

The giant replica had at least a 15-foot wingspan, almost the size of a small hang glider. Its aluminum frame made it both light and strong. Real feathers covered the entire bird. Glass eyes seemed to watch our every move. An amplified speaker was hidden in the throat. Finally, it had powerful claws that actually opened and closed. A wireless remote controlled everything. The bird was so well-designed that I couldn't understand why it had a problem flying.

"The rockets in the wings only launch the raven," Felix explained. "After that, it's basically a glider. That way when it swoops down, there's no engine noise for the microphones on the set to pick up."

"Makes sense," I said.

"Yeah, but there's one problem," Felix said. "Unless there's a good updraft—like the one that hit me today—when the raven swoops down, it stays down. That's why it slammed into Trenton Kyle yesterday."

"Sounds like it needs a second set of rockets," I observed. "They don't have to be that big, just powerful enough to give the mechanical raven a lift after the nosedive."

Felix shook his head. "Then you'd have a noise problem."

I glanced around the lab, thinking there had to be a solution. Then I remembered my dad's replica of the

Stealth bomber. The fuel packs it used were practically silent. I told Felix what I was thinking.

"It can't hurt to ask," he said.

"Too bad that's not possible. My dad's at a sales conference," I said. "Let's just use the rockets. I'm sure Dad can order more."

Felix looked doubtful. "Isn't there some way to call your dad?"

"Not that I know of," I said. "As long as the movie crew pays for the rockets, he won't mind."

"Willie, didn't losing Amanda's mouse teach you anything?" Felix questioned, his voice booming.

"Shhh!" I warned, bringing my finger to my lips. Felix's changing voice and overbearing attitude were driving me nuts. "Amanda will hear you. Now quit talking so loud."

"I can't help it," Felix said. "If I don't talk loud, all I get is falsetto."

"In that case, go with falsetto. And quit worrying about the fuel packs. I'm sure it's okay to use them." That said, I stepped from the storeroom to the front of the hobby store in search of my quarry.

The Rocket Raven 1000

Amanda stood in the boat aisle, helping someone select a model. It was Mrs. Speer, a good customer and a family friend.

That was all I needed to see. With Amanda distracted, no one would even know I was borrowing the rockets. I hurried along the wall toward the front of the store. My dad had put the Stealth bomber on display in the front window. He stored the spare rockets in a drawer underneath the window.

When I got to the window, the Stealth bomber was gone. Dad must have taken it to the conference to show other hobby enthusiasts. I couldn't blame him. It was definitely the most impressive model he'd ever built. It measured four feet across and flew with incredible accuracy.

Checking the drawer, I hoped he'd left some of the fuel cylinders behind. He had, but only four. Each cylinder wasn't much larger than a roll of quarters, but it packed plenty of power. I quickly slipped all four into my pocket as Amanda headed for the cash register.

"So when will I get to see some of your fancy ceramic work that I've been hearing about?" Mrs. Speer asked Amanda, following her to the register.

Amanda blushed. "Actually, it's not that fancy. Is it Willie?"

"Um … no. I mean, yeah." I bounced on the balls of my feet like a nervous cat burglar.

"From what I understand, you've become quite the artist," Mrs. Speer went on. "I know your mother is mighty impressed. And she's not one to exaggerate."

"Thanks," Amanda said sheepishly. "I plan to have a few things on display at the craft fair."

"I'll be looking," Mrs. Speer said as she paid for her sailboat model and headed outside.

I was just as eager to get away, but the moment the front door closed, Amanda was on me like a private eye. "Willie, you haven't seen my ceramic mouse, have you?"

"I remember seeing it yesterday. It looked great," I answered.

"Thanks. I thought I put it with the rest of my pieces, but I can't find the little guy anywhere." Amanda tapped her maroon fingernails on the glass display case. "You don't know where it could be, huh?"

I shook my head. "Um … no. I have no idea where that thing is right now. Sorry."

"Now I know how *you* feel," Amanda said. "I can't find my mouse and you can't find Biz."

I played along while inching my way toward the storeroom door. "Yeah. *Heh-heh.* What a coincidence. Well, got to get back to the lab. Catch you later."

Felix overheard part of our conversation and gave me the third degree when I joined him. "I can't believe you didn't tell her the truth."

"I didn't lie to her. I have no clue where Biz took her mouse." I put the fuel cylinders on the lab table. "Now, come on. Let's install these before Amanda comes back here to ask more questions."

Felix stared at the rockets as if they were contaminated. "Something tells me this is a big mistake."

"Quit worrying about it," I fumed. "As long as the studio pays for replacements, my dad won't care. Let's finish this."

Working together, Felix and I made a casing to place under each wing to hold the fuel cylinders. We attached the casings underneath the feathers using the strongest, lightest model glue my dad stocked.

"That ought to do it," Felix said. "Twelve hours of drying time and the mechanical raven will be ready for a test flight."

I stepped back to get the complete perspective of our enhanced bird. "Forget the *mechanical raven* stuff. From now on, this baby is the Rocket Raven 1000."

"I like the way that sounds," Felix agreed. "But what counts is what Rob thinks."

"There's only one way to find out," I said. "Tomorrow morning we'll deliver our creation to Mr. Robert Karpman, location manager for *Revenge of the Raven*. Then he'll know exactly what happens when two 13-year-old geniuses go Hollywood."

We returned to the Pike Estate the next day and found Rob near the craft services tent. One look at the Rocket Raven 1000 and his eyes almost popped out of his head. "Thanks, guys. I'm impressed. You're the best."

"Glad we could help," Felix said.

Rob directed his attention toward me. "Willie, I'm still not happy about the problem with Biz, but this is a step in the right direction.

"Speaking of which, you got another reprieve," Rob added. "The director has decided to shoot another scene that doesn't rely on the real ravens or the Rocket Raven 1000. So don't sweat the 48-hour deadline I gave you."

"Cool," I said, feeling some relief.

"It gets better," Rob went on. "Your friend Sam's in the scene, but she only has a few lines. She's ready to go."

"Good for her," I said sarcastically, still disappointed about my less-than-stellar job.

"You mean good for you. The scene calls for extras," Rob said.

"Are you kidding?" Felix asked.

"Nope. You'll just stand in the background," Rob explained. "You won't have lines or anything. But you'll still be in the movie *and* you'll get paid. Can I count on you?"

"We're in," I said. "Send the makeup artist to my trailer. I'll have a snack and wait for her there."

"Actually, you don't get a trailer. But if you would like some makeup on a cracker, I'll see what I can do." Rob said with a laugh. Then he explained my *hors d'oeuvres* fiasco to Felix. Apparently, Sam hadn't hesitated to describe my slight social mishap to anyone who would listen.

"You ate makeup on a cracker?" Felix wailed, in a half-broken, half-deep voice. "What a spazz!"

I forced a smile. "That's show business."

When Rob was done sharing the laugh with Felix, he directed us toward the porch of Colonel Pike's house for the next shoot. Crew members hurried everywhere, getting things ready.

The scene centered around Trenton Kyle. He would tell the neighborhood kids the fate of the giant oak tree and how it might impact the ravens. Our job was to pretend to listen halfheartedly and regard Trenton Kyle's fears as nonsense.

The director barked orders to the camera crew and lighting technicians. Rob adjusted old furniture on the porch, creating the perfect setting. When everything was ready to go, an assistant director moved the extras into position. He told Felix and me to lean against the porch bannister. Several kids, including Crusher Grubb, were seated beneath us.

"This is so cool," Felix said.

"Yeah. I hope they get my good side," I replied, not really knowing what my good side was.

The director stood in front of us, explaining what we were to do. "When you hear the word *background*, you're on. The main thing is to look doubtful. Your expression and body language should read: 'Sorry, Trenton, I don't buy it.' "

We all nodded.

"There's a few more things to remember," the director continued. "Number 1, don't look at the camera—no matter what. Number 2, keep your attention on Trenton Kyle. He's the one speaking to you, not me or another crew member. And number 3, be quiet. The microphones we use are extremely sensitive. Any questions?"

Before I could raise my hand, the director turned away, as if certain no one would have a question. But I did.

"Excuse me," I said. "I have a question. When do we see our contracts?"

"Extras don't get contracts. You get a check in the mail that amounts to minimum wage," the director explained. He rolled his neck as if to relieve tension and gazed skyward as if questioning why he had to put up with locals.

I couldn't believe it. No trailer, no makeup, and now no contract. What a gyp. I had to force myself not to throw a tantrum and call my agent, which could have proved difficult since I didn't have an agent. I consoled myself with the fact that at least I'd be in the movie. It was definitely a step up from birdcage cleaner.

With all the extras in position, the director called for the stars. When they arrived, his poor-me attitude changed in a hurry. "Looking good, Trenton. Beautiful, Sam. Very nice."

I thought I would gag hearing him gush all over them. To make things worse, Sam ate it up. She joked with the director like he was an old friend. And when Trenton spoke to her, she looked like she would melt.

"This is making me sick," I whispered to Felix.

"Shhh," Felix shot back. And so did Crusher Grubb.

The director told Sam to sit next to Trenton Kyle on a porch swing. "Looks good," he said. "I think we're ready."

"Okay on sound and lighting," one of the technicians called.

The camera operator also gave a thumbs-up.

"Excellent," the director said. "We're running behind, so let's try and get this on the first take." He sat down in his chair next to the camera and the other crew members.

"Stand by," one of the technicians said.

A guy with a two-piece marker board stepped in front of the camera. "*Revenge of the Raven*, porch scene, take one," he said, snapping the two halves of the board shut.

Just hearing those words made me nervous. Suddenly, I couldn't remember what the director had told us. My stomach churned. My hands tingled.

The director raised a hand. "Rolling. Background. Action."

I felt like a deer frozen in the beams of a car's headlights. I stared straight into the camera, as if drawn in by some kind of tractor beam.

"Cut!" the director yelled. "Yo, Red. You on the bannister. What'd I say about looking into the camera?"

"The name's Plummet. Willie Plummet," I replied.

"Yeah. Whatever. Keep your eyes off the camera and on Trenton," the director said.

"Sorry. My fault," I said. I caught a glimpse of Sam glaring at me. I didn't want to see the expression on Crusher's face.

"Let's try it again," the director snapped.

The guy with the wooden marker stepped in front of the camera again. He repeated his earlier performance with the addition of "Take two." He snapped the two halves of the sign together.

"Places, everyone," an assistant said.

The director bellowed his list: "Rolling. Background. Action."

This time I did much better, especially when Trenton Kyle started to speak.

"Don't you guys care about the ravens?" he asked, his voice dripping with distress.

"I do," Sam offered.

"What about the rest of you?" Trenton Kyle asked. He stood up and pleaded on behalf of the ravens. He blabbed on and on, urging us to come to their defense.

As Kyle spoke, I found myself responding with negative body language without even thinking about it. I wasn't too keen on Mr. Hunk anyway. I crossed my arms. Shook my head. Pulled my eyebrows together and squinted. Felix did the same. Sam, on the other hand, gazed at Trenton Kyle with frosty eyes, as if he were some kind of hero.

"Those ravens need our help, otherwise their home will be destroyed," Trenton urged.

I continued my Oscar-level performance, ready to roll my eyes at Kyle when something in the distance caught my attention. It couldn't be!

Is It Soup Yet?

It was. Biz glided over the corral, then swooped in our direction. It looked like he still clutched the ceramic mouse in his claw. I watched him closely, thankful that everyone in the crew was watching the porch and couldn't see him.

"Cut!" the director shouted. "Plummet, you look like you saw an angel. I said *uninterested*, not enlightened. Now let's try it again."

Rob cleared his throat threateningly in my direction. His raging eyes bored holes in my head.

"Take three," the crew member said.

"Rolling. Background. Action," the director snapped.

I did my best to look at Trenton Kyle, but with Biz flying around, it wasn't easy. I rolled my eyes, thinking I could keep track of him and look disgusted at the same time.

At least, that was my plan.

"*Caw! Caw!*" Biz called out. He landed on top of the food tent.

"Cut!" the director shouted. He jumped to his feet and turned around. "Who let that raven out? Somebody get him."

"I'm on it" I said. I sprang from the porch and ran across the yard, tearing my shirt over my head in the process. It wasn't much of a net, but it would have to do. I raced with amazing speed. Biz sat still, picking at a length of cord on top of the tent. Jumping on a picnic table, I sprang for the roof like a flying squirrel.

Too bad I weigh a smidge more than a squirrel.

As I landed on the tent's roof, the entire structure collapsed beneath me—frame, canvas, and all. Biz lifted like a helicopter. I dropped like a brick. The first thing I hit was a food table. Too bad it wasn't empty. I landed in a pot of tomato soup left over from lunch. One thing about those fancy movie caterers—they keep their food really hot.

"Yeow!" I wailed, jumping straight up. "Ouch. Ouch. Ouch."

Talk about a hot seat. My jeans dripped like steaming sponges. Food was splattered in every direction. The color of my skin matched my hair. I hopped and kicked like a kangaroo with his tail on fire, searching for relief.

I spied a large blue ice chest half-covered by the fallen tent. Pulling the canvas aside, I flipped the lid off the chest and sat on the ice inside. "Ahhh."

By the time I glanced up, the entire cast and crew were staring at me, except for Rob. He looked in the other direction as if we'd never met.

The director, on the other hand, got right in my face. "Plummet, you're killing me. First, you ruin the scene. Then you destroy craft services. Either get it together or you're fired."

I sat there, soaking in soup and ice, speechless.

The director turned his wrath on Rob. "Until the wrangler shows up, those birds are your responsibility. After all the problems we've had with that mechanical raven, I would have thought you'd do a better job of looking after the real ones."

I couldn't keep quiet any longer. I carefully climbed out of the cooler. "Actually, I'm the one who let Biz out. It was an accident. He got loose when I was cleaning the cage."

"Why am I not surprised?" the director fumed.

I stared at the soup and water pooling beneath my feet, certain of what would come next. The director would scream, "You're fired!" so loudly they'd hear it in Hollywood.

But that's not what happened.

"Well?" he growled. "What are you waiting for? Get back on the porch. If nothing else, we're going to finish this scene."

"But I'm dripping with soup," I pointed out.

"Good for you. Now get over there," the director ordered. "As soon as we finish the scene, you can track down that raven. If he doesn't come back, *you* don't come back."

Dripping my way to the porch, I sat down on the rail. My pants clung to my legs. I'd never felt so gross. Sam looked at me and shook her head. Everyone else on the crew smirked. Now I knew why the director had made me stay—punishment.

Sitting there was brutal. I've had a number of misadventures in my life, and I've been embarrassed plenty of times, but this topped them all. Instead of scoring my big movie break, I was sitting in soup-soaked jeans like some kind of oyster cracker. Show business wasn't what it was cracked up to be.

When the director said, "Action," I forced myself to follow his original instructions to the letter. I didn't make a peep, look at the camera, or even *think* about Biz. I did what I was told, and it paid off. In less than 10 minutes, we shot the scene perfectly.

"Print that one," the director called. "Excellent, Trenton. You too, Samantha. Very nice."

The extras and crew members also received their share of compliments. Felix even got a pat on the back. But not me. It was as if I didn't exist. It kind of bummed me out, but I decided that compared to getting chewed out, being ignored was just fine.

As the crew cleaned up and the extras and actors went their separate ways, I crossed the Pike Estate, eager to go home and change.

Felix caught up with me. "You should have seen yourself falling through the tent and landing in that pot of soup. You went head-to-head with the Three Stooges on that one," he said.

"Thanks. You really know how to cheer a guy up."

"Talk about hilarious," Felix squeaked, his voice cracking. "The director actually made you play that scene dripping wet. Think about it. Every time we watch *Revenge of the Raven*, we can laugh over you sitting there in soup-soaked jeans!" Felix slapped his knees and almost fell over, he was laughing so hard.

"I can hardly wait," I muttered.

For the next few blocks, Felix continued to bust up while I glared at cracks in the sidewalk, stewing. Until I could find Biz, I wasn't welcome on the set. But how could I find Biz without any bait? I had lost Amanda's only mouse. And her other ceramics wouldn't attract a raven. Too bad she didn't have more mice.

"Wait a minute," I said. I grabbed Felix's arm. "We're taking a different way home."

"Where are we going?" he asked.

"You'll see. It's only a little out of our way, but it's worth it." We turned down a street lined with shops and stopped when we got to the corner.

"A pet store?" Felix asked. "You think you can *buy* a raven?"

"Nope," I said with a smile. "But I can buy mice. Lots of real, live mice."

We headed inside and found them right away. I selected three of the plumpest squeakers I'd ever seen. "I'll call them Larry, Moe, and Curly. If these morsels don't lure Biz, nothing will."

The clerk gave me and my soup-stained jeans a weird look as he placed the mice in a cardboard box. The rodents scurried along the box's walls, twitching their whiskers and clawing the cardboard. After paying, I closed the lid and we headed outside.

"You really think those mice will do the trick?" Felix asked as we resumed our walk home.

"Absolutely," I said with a confident nod.

When we got to Felix's house, I reluctantly asked for his help in the morning. "Just make sure you pay attention this time," I said.

"If you don't want my help, I can always head over to the Pike Estate. Rob said *I'm* welcome anytime," Felix replied.

"Sure, rub it in."

As Felix disappeared inside his house, I picked up the pace and hurried home. When I got there, I raced upstairs. All I could think about was getting out of my soup-soaked jeans before Amanda and Orville saw me and tortured me for a lifetime. Leaving the mice unattended in a cardboard box probably wasn't the best idea, but I couldn't wait a moment more to get out of those jeans. I put the box on my bed and loped down the hall toward the bathroom.

"What's the rush?" Mom asked as I trotted past.

"Hard day on the set. I need to clean up."

After a hot shower and a change of clothing, I hurried back to my bedroom to check on the mice. It never occurred to me to worry. A pet store would never sell mice in a box that wasn't escape-proof.

At least that's the way I saw it. I lifted the lid.

The box was empty. I looked underneath it. Behind it. Nothing. Just a hole in one corner and a trail of droppings and cardboard pieces that led to the edge of my bed.

"Here, Moe. Here, Curly. Larry, come to Willie." *If only Felix were here*, I thought. His squeaky voice would make the perfect mouse call.

Orville poked his head inside my bedroom. "Did I just hear you calling the Three Stooges?"

"Not really the Three Stooges," I explained. "Three mice."

"They're not blind, are they?" he asked.

"Real funny," I replied. "I bought three mice to use for raven bait. Now they're gone."

"What a goofball," Orville laughed. "You'd better hope you find them before Mom and Amanda do."

"They only got loose a few minutes ago. Mom and Amanda are down in the family room. How fast do you think—"

"Aaahh!" A scream rose from beneath us, followed by the sound of something breaking. "Get away! Get away!"

"About that fast," Orville said with a grin.

I rushed past him and sped down the stairs. At the bottom I turned and bolted into the family room. Amanda stood on the coffee table, clutching two ceramic figurines as if they were her last defense.

"It's under the couch," Mom blurted at me, clinging to a bookshelf.

"Which one?" I asked.

"There's more than one?" Amanda cried.

"You bet," Orville announced, catching up with me. He told them what had happened.

"I can't believe you left them in a cardboard box!" Mom scolded. "What were you thinking?"

"I ... um ..." Realizing I had no choice, I explained what had happened with the soup. "My jeans were getting crusty. I had to get out of them."

"That's no excuse," Mom told me. "Didn't you realize that mice could chew through cardboard?"

"It would have been a pain to dig through the garage for a better container," I said.

"So you took the easy way out," Amanda concluded. "Why am I not surprised?"

Just then a mouse—Moe, I think—emerged from behind a chair and ran for the coffee table Amanda was standing on.

All I could think was, *Bad timing, Moe.* Very bad timing.

Say It Like You Mean It

"Yeow!" Amanda shrieked. She went into orbit, jumping off the coffee table and heading for the table that held her ceramics. She was too frantic to be careful. The figurines were no match for their maker. They flew in every direction as she jumped and slid to the center of the table. With her arms clutching her knees, she sat in a tightly wound ball. Broken ceramics covered the floor. Moe scurried under the couch.

Finally Mom couldn't cling to the bookshelves any longer. She bolted across the room, screaming and ran for the stairs. As she did, Curly came bouncing down the stairs straight at her.

"Ahh!" Mom wailed. She pulled a U-turn and jumped on a chair.

Curly kept going and joined Moe under the couch. With Mom and Amanda as safe as they could hope to be under the circumstances, Orville and I got on opposite ends of the couch and rolled it over.

I hoped to find the Three Stooges huddled together, but not so. Moe and Curly had disappeared. Larry was just as invisible. I dropped to my knees to look for them, searching inside the couch's springs. After a careful search, it was obvious what had happened. The Stooges had escaped through a crack in the baseboard. From there, they easily could find their way under the house.

In other words, the Three Stooges were gone. I might have felt sorry for myself if it weren't for Amanda. She had lost far more than me. And that didn't count the prize mouse I had swiped for Biz bait. For a moment I considered confessing, but I decided I was in deep enough already.

I was right. For the next 10 minutes, Mom chewed me out and told me I'd have to help pay for Amanda's broken creations. I stood quietly, not daring to argue or to offer an excuse. Getting banned from the movie set was bad enough. One ill-timed wisecrack and I feared I'd be banished from home too.

When I got into bed that night, I turned off the light, then quickly turned it back on. I felt too guilty to sleep. Opening my Bible, I decided to read the verse Felix, Sam, and I had argued about when we got involved with the movie. I remembered from youth group that it was in Matthew.

I found it: Matthew 7:13–14. It read: "Enter through the narrow gate. For wide is the gate and broad is the road that leads to destruction, and many enter through it. But small is the gate and narrow the road that leads to life, and only a few find it."

I looked at the words, confused. We'd passed through a narrow gate when we'd tried to get parts in the movie. And it had worked, especially for Sam and Felix. But there was another word that caught my eye—*wide*. That was the gate for the people who wanted a convenient way out, regardless of the consequences. Tonight, I definitely opted for the easy—and selfish—way when it came to taking care of the mice. It also had been quicker to take Amanda's mouse than ask for permission up front.

The more I thought about it, the more guilty I felt. Ever since stepping through the small gate at the Pike Estate, I had made nothing but selfish, wide-gate decisions. I remembered my youth pastor explaining that Jesus was the only way through the narrow gate. Bowing my head, I asked Him to forgive me.

"There's more to life than starring in a movie," I said out loud. Sure, it'd be cool to be a stuntman, but I had to keep things in perspective. First thing in the morning, I'd confess to Amanda. With that decided, I turned off my light again, feeling that now I'd be able to fall asleep.

The next morning when I called Felix, he seemed relieved that the mice had gotten away. "No offense, but watching Biz tear them to shreds wasn't on the top of my list."

"Mine either," I admitted, "but it's the best way I can think of to catch Biz. Now I need to buy some more. This acting stuff is getting expensive."

"Before you do, let's stop by the set. Maybe Biz went back on his own, or maybe Rob caught him," Felix said. "I'll look while you wait behind the barn. That way the director won't get on your case."

That sounded like a good idea. "Just let me tell Amanda about her ceramic mouse. Then I'll meet you behind the Pike Estate," I answered.

After hanging up I looked for my sister, mulling over how I would admit to loosing her prize creation. I checked the kitchen, the family room, and her bedroom, but I came up empty. The only family member I found was Orville. He was waxing his truck.

"She's at the hobby store, filling in for Dad," he reminded me. "And with the craft fair coming up, she's not too happy about spending 12 hours selling models. I'd stay away from her if I were you. Especially after your little mouse stunt."

My eyes bulged. "Felix told you?"

"What do you mean *Felix*? I was there, remember? Last night?"

I calmed down, realizing Orville was talking about the *real* mice. "Oh, yeah, well, thanks for the warning. I'll stay away from her."

So much for confessing. I hopped on my bike and peddled for the movie set. If Amanda was busy with customers, it wouldn't be a good time to tell her about the ceramic mouse. She was apt to throw a tantrum right there in the store, and that would be bad for business. Financially speaking, it was in the family's best interest for me to tell her later.

When I got to Colonel Pike's, I rode around to the barn to wait for Felix. He was due any minute. At least that's what I thought. When *any minute* turned into a *long time*, I decided to pay a sneak visit to Sam. It was a little risky, but once I got to her trailer, I'd be safe. If someone came by, I could hide in the bathroom.

Picking up a discarded cardboard box, I held it on my shoulder to hide my face. Walking quickly, I moved from the protection of the barn. As I headed toward Sam's trailer, I held my shoulders high and stepped with authority to give the impression that I belonged on the set.

"Delivery for Miss Stewart," I said, rapping lightly on her trailer door. When Sam didn't answer, I began to worry.

"Miss Stewart?" I asked, pounding again. Finally, the doorknob turned.

"Willie?" Sam exclaimed.

I raised a finger to my lips. "Shhh."

Sam's face brightened. "Get in here, quick. You're just the person I wanted to see."

"It's nice to feel welcome for a change," I said, stepping inside. Unfortunately, there wasn't a snack in sight. "Where's the food?"

"I ate it all. I'm so nervous I couldn't help it. Now tell me," Sam pleaded, "did you find Biz?"

"Sorry," I said with a shrug. "I had a good plan to bait him, but it didn't work out." I put down the box and peeked out the trailer window. "He didn't come back on his own?"

"No, he did not," Sam stated, obviously annoyed. "And that means I'm toast."

"Why? The director treats you like royalty."

"He won't if I don't know my lines," Sam said. "He just came by and said that this afternoon we would shoot one of two scenes. It's either Biz and Liz getting their home destroyed or me trying to convince the neighborhood kids to beware of the giant raven."

"Why not film a scene with Rocket Raven 1000? That takes the pressure off me and you," I observed.

Sam shook her head. "The director won't shoot any more scenes with the mechanical raven until the end. That way, even if someone gets hurt, all the other scenes will be done and in the vault."

"In that case, you'd better get cracking," I said, reclining on the couch, " 'Cause the Biz in show*biz* has flown the coop."

"Real funny," Sam snapped. "If I'm going to shoot this scene today, then you're going to help me." Sam handed me a copy of the script. "Here. See how I do."

I scanned the page for the beginning of her speech. "Go ahead. I'm no acting coach, but I'll try and give you a few pointers. Rolling. Action."

Sam lunged forward and pleaded with open hands. "Don't you understand? My brother saw the giant raven. You've got to believe. No one's—"

"Whoa, Sam," I said, making a *cut* motion. "You left out *him* after *believe.* It's 'You've got to believe *him.*' Now try it again. And this time concentrate."

Sam glared at me, apparently unable to handle a little constructive criticism.

I cleared my throat. "Rolling. Action."

With hands extended, Sam tried again. "My brother has seen the giant—"

"Cut," I interrupted. "It's 'My brother *saw*' not '*has seen.*' Now come on. If you can't get through the first line, how do you expect to get through a full-page monolog?"

"It's this trailer," Sam cried. "I can't get into the poor country girl mind-set cooped up in this luxury coach."

"That's a good point," I admitted. "According to the script, the location for this scene is in the barn. Let's go there."

Using my box as cover and Sam as lookout, we crept across the grounds to the barn. We had almost made it when I noticed the director standing on the porch and looking my way.

A Feathered Missile

Fortunately the box trick worked, and the director didn't recognize me. After an encouraging word to Sam, he went inside the house.

At the barn, we found the large door cracked open just enough for us to slip inside.

"Will this do?" I asked, flipping on a bare lightbulb that hung from a rafter. Bags of feed were stacked along one wall. Above us, loose hay spilled over the edge of the loft.

"It better," Sam said, looking around.

"According to the script, you stand by the door, pleading your case. The kids are sitting on the bags of feed, refusing to listen."

"Then let's try it," Sam told me.

I sat down on a feedbag with the script in my hand. This time Sam did better. To help her out, I responded just like the kids would in the scene, which wasn't hard to do. Sam spoke her lines with so little emotion, looking bored came easy.

Finally I couldn't take it any longer. "Sam, baby, you've got to spice it up a bit. The script says you're pleading with the kids. You really believe that if they ignore your brother's warning, they'll get ripped to shreds by the giant raven. This is life-or-death stuff, not a public service announcement. Now get into it."

"Willie, remember when you said you're no acting coach?" Sam asked.

"Yeah," I said, ready to soak up a compliment.

"Well, you were right. You're driving me nuts," Sam announced.

"Thanks," I said. "I'm so glad I agreed to help you."

"Oh, take it easy. I was just kidding," Sam said. After a quick glance at the script, Sam tried again, but she still delivered her lines in a monotone.

Realizing I had no other choice, I decided to show her myself. I knew the lines from staring at the script while she stumbled through it.

"I can't wait to see this," Sam grinned.

I skipped to the climax of her scene. "Why won't you believe me?" I pleaded. "My brother is trying to protect you, just like he protected me when I was a little girl."

I dropped to my knees while raising my voice for emphasis. "I was afraid of the dark, afraid of monsters under my bed. I cried over everything. But he sang to me and dried my tears," I said, a catch in my voice. "He was so brave, even when I was a—"

"Chicken," a loud voice said, then laughed. Crusher Grubb sat up in the loft. "Nice speech, Plummet. Would you like a skirt to go with that script?"

"I'm helping Sam practice," I shot back.

"Sure you are," he said, still laughing. He flopped over and held his gut, mocking me with his words. "I was *afraid* of the dark. I *cried* over everything."

"Just ignore him," Sam urged me.

Crusher loved that. "What a sissy. What a girly-boy!"

I bit my lip, realizing that when Crusher hit the streets with his news, I'd never hear the end of it. Then I saw a way to get even. A lever on the wall controlled the loft's trapdoor. A quick pull of the handle and Crusher would drop like an over-stuffed sack of grain.

Sam shook her head, realizing what I was thinking. Something told me I should turn the other cheek and walk away. But I couldn't. I had to get even.

"Hey, Lenny," I said, "have you ever heard the expression 'What goes up, must come down'?" Before Crusher could answer, I pulled the handle and watched him drop like Humpty Dumpty.

As he climbed to his feet, I slid through the barn door and headed outside.

"Plummet, you're dead!" he screamed after me.

"Plummet?" the director asked, coming across the grounds. "What are you doing here?"

"Leaving," I said over my shoulder. Or so I thought. After a few more steps, I bumped into Felix and we both tumbled to the ground.

"Oh, fine, so *now* you show up," I said, rubbing my chin.

Before we could stand, Crusher and the director were standing over us.

"Plummet, I'm going to—" Crusher began.

"Easy now," the director said, holding off Crusher. "I won't have the cast or crew fighting."

"Since when is Crusher in the cast?" I asked the director.

"I'm an extra, remember?" Crusher stated, cocking his head. "By the way, have any good soup lately?"

When the director chuckled, Crusher decided he was even for now and walked away. Rising to my feet, I patted the dust from my jeans.

The director put his hand on my shoulder. "Plummet, I'm giving you one more chance. Now get out there and find Biz. Until you do, don't come back."

I spent the rest of the day wandering around Glenfield, at times not sure whose yard I was in or which street I was on. *Find Biz?* I asked myself. At the rate I was going, someone would have to find me. I scoured the town and surrounding area like a pirate searching for treasure—only I didn't have a map. The

only bird I spotted that even looked like Biz turned
out to be a crow.

In desperation I tried calling Biz. *"Caw! Caw!"* I
called while walking from yard to yard. People looked
at me like I was nuts—something many of our neigh-
bors already suspected. A man with a cane asked me
if I was feeling okay. It didn't help much when I
explained why I was imitating a raven.

"Sorry. Haven't seen a raven named Biz all day,"
the man told me. "But my neighbor has a parrot you
can talk to. His name is Squeaky."

"Your neighbor's name is Squeaky?" I asked. The
man just laughed.

I kept walking, even more discouraged than
before. But I didn't give up. Every time I saw a garden
with vegetables or an alley with garbage, I checked
for Biz. Too bad he never appeared.

The next day I began my search on the Pike
Estate, hanging on to the slim hope that Biz might
have come back on his own.

When I got within sight of the barn, I stopped and
rubbed my eyes. "Is that Biz or his long-lost giant
brother?" I asked aloud.

A raven, or some kind of big black bird, sat on a post next to the giant oak tree. Running ahead, I noticed Felix and Rob crouching not too far from the bird. Suddenly, it all made sense. They were ready to test the Rocket Raven 1000.

"Wait up!" I yelled, running toward them.

Felix waved me over. "Hurry, we're almost out of time." When I reached them, I started to chew them out for holding a test flight without me.

Rob turned the lecture on me. "The director wants this thing ready, just in case. He doesn't want to use it until the end, but it's getting harder to find scenes to shoot. Sam's having trouble with her part, which shifts the pressure to me."

"And me," I added. "There's still no sign of Biz."

"No offense, Willie," Rob told me, "but we've got bigger fish to fry than Biz. The climax of the movie hinges on a giant raven that swoops down and carries people away."

"Then let's try it," I said, thankful that the test would take place away from the set.

"Mission control ready," Rob said, holding the remote.

Felix pushed down on the launch lever. An ignition charge traveled to the fuel packs. "We have contact," Felix announced.

In a burst of light, the Rocket Raven 1000 launched into the air like a feathered missile.

"I sure hope your modifications work," Rob said.

Felix gave me a nervous glance, then spoke in falsetto. "So do we."

Once the fuel packs gave out, the Rocket Raven turned back toward earth. Using the remote, Rob opened the wingspan to its full 15 feet. Spiraling and swooping, the Rocket Raven floated like a real bird. Its cawing sound filled the sky.

"Looks good to me," I said.

"The test is when it gets near the ground," Rob explained. He moved the giant claws into strike position. "It has always flown well at higher altitudes."

"Then let's bring it down," Felix suggested. "When it swoops to within a few feet of the ground, we'll hit the Stealth fuel cylinders. The Rocket Raven should climb again."

"As quiet as a dove," I added. "Those fuel packs are custom-made for silence."

"Let's hope so," Rob said. "But there's more to it than silence. What we need is accuracy ... and I forgot to bring out a target."

Felix searched around for something that would work. "Willie can stand out there," he suggested.

"Me?" I protested. "That thing already knocked me out of the oak tree."

"He's right," Rob said, coming to my defense. "I wouldn't want something to happen to the Rocket Raven if it crashed into Willie again."

Okay, so maybe he hadn't come to *my* defense, but at least I got out of being a target.

"I should have brought some cones to put in the grass," Rob said. "There's some by the properties truck. Felix, will you go look? I'd ask Willie, but ..."

"You don't need to explain," Felix said. As the Rocket Raven soared overhead, Felix went for cones.

When Felix didn't return, Rob got impatient. "If Sam didn't get her lines down, the director will be looking for me at any minute, wanting this raven." We waited a little longer while Rob used updrafts to keep the Rocket Raven 1000 high overhead.

"Whatever adjustments you and Felix made to the wings are paying off," Rob said. "It handles much nicer."

"Cool," I said, thankful to finally get some encouragement.

"It looks like your experience with model rockets and gliders is really paying off." Rob glanced toward the barn. "Felix should have been back by now. What's keeping him?"

"Beats me," I said. "You want me to go look for him?"

"No. If the director sees you walking around, we'll all be in trouble." Rob shoved the remote in my hand. "Here, you keep an eye on the Rocket Raven. But be careful with it. I'll go find Felix."

I stared at the remote, knowing I held far more than the controls to a giant mechanical bird. The entire movie depended on me keeping the feathered glider in the air.

Not a problem, I thought. I can do this—I made the Skyrunner 1000. Thanks to helium balloons and well-positioned propellers, that thing soared forever. People even thought it was a UFO from Planet X. Keeping the Rocket Raven 1000 in the air, while pulling off a few trick maneuvers, would be a cinch.

Working the controls, I turned the tail feathers. The Rocket Raven 1000 angled to the right and circled around me like a tetherball at the end of a rope. Turning again, I brought the Rocket Raven over the barn. I hoped the director would see it. That would score some points for Rob. It would also buy me some more time to catch Biz.

When someone came around the barn, I figured my plan had worked. Until I saw who it was. It was Trenton Kyle. Apparently he hadn't seen the mechanical raven. He had a script in his hand and was practicing his lines.

As the Rocket Raven 1000 swooped overhead, a thought came to mind. If I could impress Trenton Kyle with my maneuvering of the giant bird, maybe he would put in a good word for me with the director. Maybe I'd be a stuntman after all.

Turning the Rocket Raven toward the barn, I lowered the wing feathers to make it drop. Trenton Kyle still didn't see it. The only time he looked up from the script was to blurt out a line. I moved the Raven into position. Easy now. A gust of wind moved the bird off course, but I carefully brought it back. Another hundred yards and we'd have contact. Not literally *contact*, but close enough. The key would be turning on the Stealth fuel cylinders at just the right time.

I zeroed in. The raven cruised to within 20 feet of the ground. I set the "caw" sound for max volume. The raven would sound off just a few feet from Trenton. Only 50 more yards and the Hollywood Hunk would get the surprise of his life. Or so I thought.

Trenton Kyle looked up just as I hit the Stealth fuel cylinders.

"Aaahh!" he wailed.

As the raven zipped toward his head, Trenton looked like a terrified field mouse in the sights of a ravenous hawk.

"*Caw! Caw!*" the Rocket Raven 1000 called out.

Dropping the script, Trenton stood there, petrified. With the fuel burning silently, the raven approached at the speed of light. It zipped over Trenton's head, its talons just missing his scalp.

Now for the real test, I thought. Adjusting the controls, I guided the raven into the clouds. Perfect. The fuel packs did just what we needed them to do. The raven climbed after the initial dive and hardly made a sound in the process.

Trenton watched the bird fly, his mouth dropping open in awe. Now his expression revealed more admiration than fear. My plan had worked. But just to make sure, I decided to give Trenton one more sample of the Rocket Raven 1000. And my timing couldn't have been better. As I directed the raven for another pass, Felix and Rob reappeared.

"*Caw! Caw!*" the raven sounded off as it dropped.

I adjusted the controls for a breeze, determined to keep on track. I hoped the fuel packs would hold.

This time Trenton would really be impressed. Or so I thought. Instead, Trenton panicked and ran for the corral on the side of the barn.

Time to back off. Otherwise Trenton might have me kicked off the film for good. But before I could make the adjustment, the fuel packs ran out.

"Mayday! Mayday!" I hollered.

The Rocket Raven bore down on Trenton. Twenty feet. Ten.

Trenton jumped for the safety of the corral just as I cranked up on the wings and tail. The Rocket Raven

1000 cleared the top rail by a feather. With Trenton safe, my attention shifted to landing the gliding bird.

"Come on, big fella," I said, hoping the wing adjustments Felix and I had made would do the trick. I pulled back on the controls, watching.

It worked! The Raven gained altitude. Not a lot, but enough to bring it around. All my years of flying model planes with my dad were paying off. By making slight changes in the angles of the wings and tail feathers, I guided the Rocket Raven just where I wanted it. Keeping the bird about six feet off the ground, I waited until it was practically to me. Then I turned it straight up. The raven lifted a few feet, then stalled, ready to drop.

Stepping underneath the raven, I raised my arm and grabbed it by the claws.

Felix and Rob stared in awe, their mouths hanging open. I took a bow as they applauded and jogged toward me. I handed the Rocket Raven 1000 and controls to Rob, then gave Felix a high five.

Too bad Trenton Kyle wasn't quite so eager to celebrate. He climbed out of the corral, fit to be tied. He was black with mud and manure.

I tried to make light of it. "I thought mud packs were the rage in Hollywood. It's supposed to help the complexion or something."

"A mud pack, yes. A mud sty, no," Rob explained. "There's a difference."

"In that case, it's time for me to exit—stage right. Later, guys." With that, I took off running, hoping I could get away from Trenton Kyle as fast as the Rocket Raven 1000 had just flown.

When I got home, I figured that Amanda would be at the hobby store filling in for my dad. But Orville had agreed to cover for her so she could work on her ceramics. The big show was just two days away.

Maybe it was a sense of confidence that came from the Rocket Raven's successful flight. Or maybe it was just guilt. But I decided to tell Amanda that I'd lost her prize mouse in a failed effort to catch Biz.

Amanda and Mom sat at a table in the family room. Amanda was applying the finishing touches to a small family of squirrels. At first I couldn't help but wonder if they would make good Biz bait. I quickly put that thought out of my mind.

"I can't believe how good you are at this," I said, picking up one of the baby squirrels. "Your display will be the best at the show." I hoped that a compliment would soften Amanda for the news to come.

"You mean the smallest," Amanda said. "First, my mouse disappeared. Then, thanks to your Three Stooges mice trick, half my pieces were smashed."

So much for softening her up. Suddenly, the act of confessing got harder. But I couldn't call it off. I silently asked Jesus for some help and jumped back in. "Well, you know what they say: *It's quality, not quantity, that counts.*"

Amanda stopped working and glared at me. "Are you saying the ones that broke *weren't* quality?"

"Um … no. That's not what I meant. It's just that with fewer pieces, the ones you *do* have will get more attention."

Mom glanced at me. "Willie, maybe you should find something else to do," she suggested.

"I wish I could." I explained that Felix and Sam were still on the movie set and that, because of Biz, I was unwelcome.

"You still haven't caught that raven?" Amanda asked. She held an Exacto knife like a pen, etching tiny lines resembling fur in the squirrel's tail.

"No, and believe me, I've tried everything." I swallowed hard, deciding to go for it. The knife in Amanda's hand caused my voice to rise a few notes. "For instance, when Biz first escaped, I um … sort of used … um … this bait I thought would like—"

"What are you talking about?" Amanda asked, growing impatient. She and Mom watched me closely.

"A fake mouse," I blurted out. "I used a fake mouse to lure Biz."

Amanda rose to her feet, putting two and two together. "What kind of *fake* mouse?" she asked.

"A ceramic one," I squeaked.

"You used my ceramic mouse for bait?" Amanda roared. She sounded like a mama bear that had just lost her cubs.

Hot-Wired

I tried to get away, but Amanda leapt halfway across the room, still holding the Exacto knife. She clutched her maroon fingernails around my arm. "Tell me you're joking!" she demanded.

"Sorry," I gasped, wincing. "I never thought Biz would steal it."

My mom came over and pried the knife from Amanda's hand. "Not that you would use this, honey, but it makes me uncomfortable."

"No problem, Mom," Amanda said sweetly. Then she looked at me and the mama bear look returned. "How could you just take it without asking?"

"I said I was sorry," I repeated and explained what had happened, but it only made things worse.

"When I asked you in the store where it was, you said you didn't know!" Amanda said accusingly. She tightened her grip.

"I didn't know," I gasped. "And I still don't."

After a final squeeze, Amanda let go. I rubbed my arm, trying to get some circulation going again. My burning face felt as red as my hair. Struggling forward, I sat down on the couch.

Mom took that as her cue to pick up where Amanda had left off. "You may not know where that mouse is now, but you will. Search every square inch of this town until you find it," she ordered.

"But, Mom, I've already—"

"I don't want to hear it. Now get going."

I got going. But I had only made it to the back door when the phone rang. Whoever it was wanted to talk with me. My mom said I couldn't come to the phone. After talking a little more, she hung up.

"That was Felix calling from the Pike Estate," she explained. "He says he just saw Biz flying around the set. He's not sure, but he thinks he may have seen a ceramic mouse in his claws. If I were you, I'd get over there, pronto."

That was all I needed to hear. As the screen door slammed behind me, I took off in a full sprint for the movie set. Running through the neighborhood, I couldn't believe how fast the celebration over the Rocket Raven had ended. But at least a burden had been lifted from my shoulders. It felt good to have confessed to Amanda, even though the consequences meant living in the streets and fields of Glenfield until I found that mouse.

Now I had the opportunity to catch Biz and find the mouse. In a sense, I'd kill two birds with one stone, though I felt a little uncomfortable using that analogy. By now the fake mouse would probably be a little scratched up, but with a quick paint job, it would be as good as new.

I reached downtown and slowed to a jog. I gasped for air but kept going, past my dad's store and other shops, until I made it to Colonel Pike's street. I crept through the movie lot as quietly as I could, making sure to keep the trailers between myself and the movie crew.

Scrambling from telephone pole to shrub to tree, I worked my way to the back of the house. Crouching low, I peered around the corner to check the layout of the place and see what was happening. From all the cables leading into the barn, it was clear that Sam's big scene had begun.

That was perfect for me. With the director and everyone else in the barn, I could roam the grounds looking for Biz. Making my way past the craft services tent, I checked the house and looked around each of the trailers. No Biz.

I stopped by his cage, hoping he had come back to visit Liz. But she was all alone, pecking at the wire cage and looking miserable.

"I think it's time you talked Biz into coming home," I told her.

"*Caw! Caw!*" Liz said in return.

Next I searched through every tree on the grounds and along the street. Biz was nowhere to be found. Felix wasn't around either. I listened for his extra-loud voice—sometimes high, sometimes low—but that didn't help. A few crew members wearing headphones ran in and out of the barn, but that was it. Apparently Biz had taken off soon after Felix had seen him.

As a last-ditch effort, I decided to look in the field. Maybe Biz had returned to where we had first baited him.

Wrong again. The field was empty and so was the giant oak tree. Leaning against the old oak, I tried to figure out what to do. With so much happening in the barn, I wanted to forget about Biz and watch the shoot. But if I did that, I could forget about going home tonight. Besides, one look from the director and I'd be toast.

I had to keep looking for Biz. But where? Felix said he'd seen him. But where was Felix at the time? And for that matter, where had Felix gone? Then it hit me. The barn!

Felix must have been in the barn helping Rob with the shoot. Could Biz have been in there too? It made sense. He was used to being indoors. And ravens were known for going into barns to find mice or to eat stored grain. In fact, the movie's plot was based on a raven that ate growth hormones while in a barn.

I jogged around to the back of the barn and found a knothole to look through. Sam was in the center of everything, speakng her lines. The camera was rolling. Everyone was perfectly silent. Hot lights lit up the barn. The sound guy wore headphones and sat twisting dials at a mixing console. The camera operator sat perched behind the camera, which was on a hydraulic lift.

Everything and everyone was right there ... including Biz! He sat just a few feet away, on the other side of the wall. But no one saw him. The crew was watching Sam. Biz perched quietly right behind them.

"You're mine now, Biz baby," I whispered. The second the shoot ended, I'd go in and catch that overstuffed blackbird. He'd have no way out. The only thing that made me uneasy was his roost. Biz was sitting on one of the power cables I'd seen earlier. It was a thick cable that ran from the Grip and Electric truck to a transformer in the barn.

"Be careful, big guy," I whispered, wondering how many volts were passing under Biz's feet.

No sooner had I spoken than Biz leaned over and pecked at the cable.

"*Psst*," I hissed, hoping to distract him. Sam's voice, thick with emotion, filtered through the barn's wooden sides.

Biz turned to look at me, then pecked the cable again. That really got me angry. I was tempted to let Mr. Featherbrain fry. But I couldn't or I'd be fried, so

I decided to try another approach. I tossed a pebble through the knothole. Instead of hitting Biz, the rock hit an electrician. I ducked just as he turned. *If nothing else*, I thought, *he'll see Biz and grab him.* Wrong again.

When I looked again, the crew member was pushing the guy next to him. Biz was pecking away at the cable for all he was worth. At that rate, he'd be through the rubber coating in no time. Then it'd be rotisseried raven for dinner. I had to do something before it was too late. Running from the barn, I traced the cable to the truck.

"Here goes nothing," I said. Grabbing hold, I yanked the giant cable free.

Shouts erupted from the barn as everyone tried to find their way to the door in the dark. When the door flew open, the cast and crew poured out, squinting into the bright sunlight. That was my cue. I navigated through the crowd into the barn. But Biz was on alert. He flew past me and out the door before I could grab him.

"Don't tell me," the director said, putting his trembling hand on my shoulder. "Plummet pulled the plug."

"I'm really sorry," I said with a sigh. "But I had to or Biz would have been fried."

"Plummet, look around," the director said. "Right now Biz is the only one *not* fried on this set."

Looking at the sea of angry faces, I had to agree.

That night I sat in my room, staring out the window. It was a long shot, but I prayed that Biz would fly up to the glass. I'd simply open up the window and let him inside. That easy.

But instead of Biz, I got shooting stars. One, then another, flashed through the black distance. In a surprising way, that helped. I figured if God held the stars in His hand, as fast as they were traveling, He held Biz too. Things would work out.

For a long time I watched the stars and prayed, and not just for a way to catch Biz. As difficult as the Lord's path was sometimes, I knew I wanted to be there.

I asked Jesus to help me always use the small gate, just like He did. He didn't crumble when tempted. He didn't back down when His enemies opposed Him. He went to the cross to pay the price for our sins, even though He had never sinned, not even once. He gave His life so I would receive forgiveness and eternal life. Talk about an incredible accomplishment! There was nothing easy about it.

The more I thought about what Jesus had done for me, the more ashamed I felt for how much I'd been goofing up lately.

Then the phone rang. It was Sam.

"You're still speaking to me?" I asked in amazement. "Didn't I ruin your big scene?"

"Just one take. After that, I was so mad at your blunder, intense emotion came easy. The director couldn't stop talking about how impressed he was."

"Glad I could help," I said dismally.

"Good, because your help is needed now more than ever," Sam said. "With my big scene done, there's not much left to shoot. It's up to you, Willie. Catch Biz or else."

From encouragement to ultimatum, how nice. I was starting to think that *or else* was all I would ever hear. Not that I had anyone to blame but myself. After taking the easy way out time and time again, I deserved what I was getting.

Speaking of which, as soon as I hung up, my dad came home. Everyone gathered around him in the family room to hear about the conference. Amanda made a special effort to sit on the opposite side of the room from me. She refused to even look in my direction, and I knew that she couldn't wait to tell Dad what I'd done with her mouse. That made me remember the Stealth fuel packs that I had "borrowed" from the shop. I decided it might be best if I went back to my room.

When I got up to leave, my dad motioned for me to sit. "Hold on, Willie. You'll want to hear this."

Reluctantly, I sat down near the door.

Carrion Casserole

Dad oozed with enthusiasm. "At the conference, I met the organizers of this weekend's craft fair. They had come to recruit hobby enthusiasts to set up booths at the fair," Dad said. "Traditionally, females make up the majority of those who attend the fair. The organizers want to expand the fair to include the whole family. They think displays that feature model cars and planes will do the trick."

"Sounds like a good plan," Mom said.

"That's what I thought," Dad said. "I told them that Plummet's Hobbies would be there. And I gave them a demonstration of the Stealth bomber. When they saw it in action, they begged me to fly it at the craft fair. If anything will appeal to guys, the Stealth will."

I could have croaked on the spot. It was too unbelievable. "Dad, did you say the Stealth bomber?"

My dad nodded with pride. "That's right. Talk about an opportunity. Half the town will be there," he said. "Who knows? Maybe some of the movie people will see my custom-made Stealth bomber in action."

"Actually, they probably see that kind of thing all the time," I reasoned. "If I were you, I'd fly one of your World War II models. The nostalgia angle might really impress them."

Amanda protested right off. "No, I agree with Dad. The Stealth bomber is his prize creation. If he's going to put something in the fair, it really should be his *best work*," she pointed out. "At least that's how I would want it. My best work. Wouldn't you agree, Willie?"

"This could only happen to me," I complained. After a long sigh, I asked Jesus to help me take the narrow gate and confess. "Dad, I sort of used some of your Stealth bomber fuel packs."

"You what?" My dad choked on the words.

As he sat in silent shock, I explained what had happened. I hoped that the successful flight of the Rocket Raven 1000 would temper his anger. Boy, was I wrong.

"Willie, how could you do that?" Dad demanded. "You know better than that."

"I would have asked, but you were gone," I said.

"Why didn't you call me?"

"At the conference?" I asked.

"Yes! They could have paged me," Dad said. "I used six fuel cylinders at the conference. I was planning on using the remaining four at the fair."

"Can't you just order more?" I asked.

"Not now! There's not enough time." Veins bulged in my dad's temples as he stood up and paced. "First thing in the morning, you go get the rockets back."

I couldn't imagine telling Rob we needed the fuel packs back, so I tried another angle. "What if they buy them from you? I'm sure they'd pay a lot."

My dad shook his head. "It's not about money. I made a commitment to the fair organizers to fly the Stealth bomber, and I intend to keep it."

By the time my dad was done chewing me out, I could barely lift my head. Once I got back to my room, I returned to my position in front of the window. The stars were still there, which helped. As bad as I felt, at least I knew God was still in control and just as able to work things out. Confessing to my dad was painful, but I knew taking the easy way out would have hurt a lot more.

⁓∽⁓

The next morning, I was in the shower when Rob called. He left a message for me to call him back, but I couldn't, not until I caught Biz. Asking for the jet packs back would be hard enough; I wanted some good news to go along with it.

Felix called next, and I was tempted to jump back into the shower to avoid his call too. Lately, all he had was bad news. But this time he surprised me.

"Willie, I stayed up reading last night, just for you," Felix informed me.

"Don't tell me," I said, "you found a Bible verse that predicts disaster for goofballs like me."

"Actually I was reading about ravens," Felix said. "I hoped to discover a fresh idea to help catch Biz."

"Well?" I asked.

"Supposedly, they're not picky eaters. They eat small rodents, grains, vegetables, even carrion."

"Carrion?" I said. "You mean that expensive delicacy made from fish eggs?"

"No, Brainiac. That's caviar. Carrion is dead flesh, like roadkill."

"Sick."

"I'm only telling you what I found," Felix said.

"Thanks for trying," I said. "But so far Biz seems more interested in watching the crew shoot scenes than in eating."

A silence followed as we both tried to come up with a plan to catch the wayward raven.

Felix sighed. "Maybe you should just—"

"Wait a second," I interrupted. "I've got it. The perfect plan. It's guaranteed to work."

"Here we go again," Felix said with a sigh.

"I'm serious, Felix," I said.

"So am I."

"Just grab some fruit from craft services, then meet me in the field behind the Pike Estate. I'll fill you in when I get there." With that, I picked up some leather gloves and bolted to meet Felix. I felt guilty about not calling Rob back, but I decided I would see him soon enough.

Felix was in the field when I arrived, holding a bunch of grapes. As I approached, he watched me with suspicion. "Well? Let's hear it."

"We know that ravens eat carrion," I reminded him. "We also know that Biz, as a veteran bird actor, loves to watch other actors at work."

Felix crossed his arms. "Yeah, what's your plan?"

I slipped on the glove and squeezed Felix behind the neck. "What we need is a death scene."

"Whose death?" Felix asked.

"Yours of course. That's why you brought the fruit: to choke on," I explained. "The grapes that drop around you will serve as the appetizer."

Felix laughed. "Wait a second. You want me to stumble around, gagging, until I collapse on the ground? Then I'm supposed to lie perfectly still until Biz swoops down, perches on my face, and plucks out my eyeballs?"

"Exactly," I said with enthusiasm. "Except for the eyeball part. That's going a little too far."

"That's got to be the most preposterous plan you've ever come up with," Felix said.

I raised my hands. "Don't start bagging on me yet. First, we've got to see if it works."

Felix dug in his heels. "Forget it. I'm no actor."

I put an arm across his shoulders. "This isn't Broadway. Just give it a try," I encouraged.

After more complaining, Felix reluctantly agreed to go along with my plan. Soon we were ready to start. I squatted in a bush near the oak tree. "Rolling. Background. Action."

Our timing couldn't have been better. As if answering my call, Biz rose from a cluster of trees in the distance and circled overhead. He looked smaller than I remembered him.

"He must be hungry, Felix," I observed. "Look how much weight he's lost."

Felix ignored me, trying to get into his character. He popped a few grapes in his mouth, then grabbed his throat and thundered, "Help! I'm choking!"

"Shhh," I whispered. "That's too loud. You'll scare him off."

Felix shook his head, then started again. I waited for Biz to drop, but he didn't. He continued to circle high overhead. No wonder. This time Felix sounded like a squeaky robot—a robot that couldn't act.

"Ham it up a little," I whispered.

"Air! I need air! The grapes were poisoned. And sour too." Felix staggered back and forth for effect.

Poisoned and sour? A scriptwriter Felix was not. Amazingly enough, it worked. Biz dropped suddenly, hovering less than 20 feet above us. It looked like my chance to right my wrong had finally come.

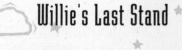

Felix noticed Biz and collapsed in the tall grass beside me. He finished his theatrical turn by closing his eyes and sticking out his tongue.

Nice touch, Felix, I thought. Too bad Biz didn't think so. He flew to a branch in the oak tree and started cleaning his feathers.

"Ut wong?" Felix asked, his tongue still extended.

"You died too soon," I whispered. "Biz wasn't impressed. Or convinced for that matter. He knows you're not dead."

"I thought you said this wasn't Broadway."

"Broadway, no. Hollywood, yes. Remember, Biz makes a living as an actor. He's used to working with professionals," I said.

"*Caw! Caw!*" Biz said, his voice full of cheer.

"He's laughing at me," Felix complained.

"He's not laughing at you, he's laughing with you," I reasoned.

"But I wasn't trying to be funny."

"Really? You should have seen yourself. Now get up and try it again," I said. "And this time put some feeling into it."

Felix reluctantly complied, acting the whole death scene over again. This time Biz didn't even budge.

"You call that acting?" I growled in disgust. "One more strike and you're out. Remember, you're not Felix Patterson. You're a young Academy Award hopeful."

"Forget you," Felix shot back in a broken voice. He climbed to his feet and stomped toward the barn. "This isn't going to work. I quit."

Crawling from under the bush, I called after him, but he kept going. Biz watched Felix disappear behind the barn, then resumed cleaning his feathers.

"Willie Plummet," I said to myself. "It's up to you now. Man against beast. Go for it!"

I picked up several grapes and squeezed the juice on my face and hair. Then I popped one in my mouth and began to chew, all the while keeping an eye on Biz.

"*Ack!* ... I'm choking," I gagged. I took deep breaths, as if gasping for air. I staggered back and forth. With a trembling hand, I reached for something to hold me up. "Good-bye cruel world."

I doubled over, then straightened up again. I clasped my fists against my gut, performing the Heimlich maneuver on myself.

"Parting is such sweet sorrow," I said to Biz. Wheeling around, I dropped to my knees. "To be or not to be, that is the question."

"*Caw!*" Biz offered in response, no doubt moved by my woeful last stand.

But I wasn't through. I rose to my feet, tripped over a dirt clod, then crumbled to my knees again. I fell face first in the dirt. But I didn't stop there. I rolled over and kicked spastically. "I can't breath. Biz, help me! I beg you, Biz!"

Biz responded by jumping from his branch. He swooped over me, then circled low.

That was all I needed. I closed my eyes and crunched myself into a ball on the ground. Soon I heard grass crunching nearby. Biz apparently had landed and was preparing to dine on my eyeballs.

"Ashes to ashes. Dust to dust," I choked softly. "With a kiss, I die."

I let out a heavy groan, then shook my arms and legs for good measure. Lying still, I held my breath, waiting for Biz to land on my chest.

But that's not what I got.

"Bravo!" a familiar voice announced.

"Here! Here!" another chanted, followed by a burst of applause.

I opened my eyes to see Rob, Felix, Sam, and the director, clapping and laughing.

I stood up, not sure if I should hide behind the oak tree or take a bow. Then I remembered the point of my performance: Biz. I searched the sky, trees, and grass, but Biz was nowhere to be found.

"No!" I screamed, dropping to me knees.

"Please, no more," the director begged. "I can't take it."

"I'm not acting," I protested. "I was *this* close to catching Biz, and you guys scared him away."

"Biz?" Rob questioned. "He came back an hour ago. When the wrangler arrived, he let out a call and Biz flew right to him. That's why I called you this morning. The bird you saw must have been a crow."

"I thought it looked sort of small and mangy," I said.

For an awkward moment the group just stared at me. Then they all busted up again.

"Oh, real funny," I said, picking up some grapes. "You guys just don't know good acting when you see it." That busted them up even more.

Time to fight back, I decided. I pelted them with grapes.

"No, please don't hurt us," Rob teased.

"Yes, we'll go," the director said between gasps of laughter. "Parting is such sweet sorrow."

That really sent their laugh track into orbit. As they turned to leave, they could barely walk.

Sitting alone, I shook my head in frustration. But at least Biz was back. Now all I had to do was tell Rob that they couldn't use my dad's Stealth bomber fuel packs. Good thing they'd enjoyed a good laugh because what I was about to say wouldn't be quite so funny.

I was right.

"You've got to be kidding!" Rob protested. "Sorry, Willie, but those fuel packs belong to the production company now."

"No, they don't," I argued. "They weren't mine to give in the first place. They are my dad's. And he needs them back."

Rob grumbled and looked around. "I don't believe this. What am I supposed to tell the director?"

"The truth," I said. "It may not be the easy way out, but it's the right way."

"In that case, why don't you tell him," Rob suggested.

"Me, huh?" I swallowed hard.

Rob nodded. "Go ahead. But don't stand too close to him. He may explode."

The director didn't explode, but he came close enough. "Take them back? You're crazy! Rob bragged for hours about the modifications to the Robot Raven."

"You mean the *Rocket* Raven 1000."

"Whatever!" the director shouted. "I don't care what it's called! I care how it flies! The climax of the movie depends on that thing."

I followed the director around as he stomped between the trailers. "With the wing adjustments we made," I pointed out, "it may not even need the fuel cylinders."

"Maybe not. But we can't risk that," the director told me. As he continued to rant and rave, I apologized in every way imaginable. Rob just stood to the side.

When the director finally ran out of things to say, I went to retrieve the fuel packs. He told me to come back as soon as I got them. In the meantime, he chewed out Rob.

When I returned, they were still talking, but the director had calmed down.

"All set," I said, holding up the fuel cylinders.

The director looked at them like he was coveting two roles of gold coins.

"Well," I continued, "I guess it's time for me to go. And don't worry, I won't come back."

"Actually," the director said, "we may have something for you after all."

I stopped walking. "Really?"

He nodded. "With the wrangler here and Biz back, we can wrap up our shoot of the live ravens today. All that leaves is the big finish with the mechanical raven. We'll get that tomorrow. Would you like to help?"

"Sure! As long as I'm not cleaning the birdcage again."

"No, no," the director assured me. "This time you'll be in front of the camera and *not* just as an extra."

"Sounds awesome," I said. "But what about the Rocket Raven 1000? If you're not sure it will—"

"Don't worry about it," the director cut in. "Rob will take care of the mechanical bird. We just need to know if you're interested."

"Definitely. What's my part?" I asked.

Rob started to answer but the director stepped on his foot. "Let's just say, your part is critical," the director explained. "Can we count on you?"

"Absolutely," I said. "And I don't even care if I get my own trailer."

"Good, because you don't," the director said. He had one of his assistants get me a liability release form. "Have one of your parents sign this and bring it with you tomorrow."

"No problem," I told him. The form said something about the production company not being responsible if I got hurt, even if there was gross negligence involved. That made me a little uneasy. I doubted my mom would sign it. But I figured Dad would since he loved a good adventure as much as I did.

Moving on, the director began rounding everyone up for the scene at the oak tree. People appeared from every direction, grabbing equipment and carrying it into the field. Soon Trenton Kyle emerged from his trailer and gave me a dirty look.

Since I was obviously on his bad list, I started to leave. But Rob caught me and told me to stick around and watch the shoot. "Just stay out of the way," he said as he walked away.

I took his advice—and was glad I did. Not only did I keep from causing any problems, but I got to see Liz and Biz in action. The wrangler, who wore tan khakis and a safari hat, handled the ravens as if they were puppets. They squawked on cue as the chainsaw cut into the tree. Liz stayed put on her eggs while Biz dive-bombed the guy with the saw. Crusher Grubb and the other kids jeered the ravens. Trenton Kyle pushed the kids away and urged the men bringing down the tree to stop.

Before the tree fell, the wrangler summoned Liz to her cage. He put a dummy raven on the nest in place of Liz. At the director's signal, the chainsaw brought down the tree with Biz flying around it, cawing for his mate. But she refused to leave her eggs until it was too late. A branch crushed the dummy raven as the tree hit the ground.

"Excellent!" the director shouted. "Very nice."

Everyone cheered and complimented one another on a job well-done. With only one scene to go, everyone breathed a sigh of relief.

After shaking several hands and making a special effort to encourage Sam, I decided to head for home. Before I got too far, the wrangler caught up with me.

"Hold on a minute," he said.

I immediately tried to apologize for what had happened to Biz.

"Don't worry about it," the wrangler told me. "I heard you tried hard to catch him. Besides, Liz probably enjoyed the extra space."

I sighed with relief.

"Anyway, that's not why I came over," the wrangler said. "Someone said this might belong to you."

"What?" I asked.

He placed a ceramic mouse in my hand. "Biz brought it to me when he came back."

I just stared at the mouse in awe. Except for a few scratches, it was fine. I couldn't believe it.

"Is it yours?" he asked.

"Actually, it's my sister's. You don't know how happy this will make her," I answered.

"Glad I could help," the wrangler said. He returned to the crew.

As I walked home, I clasped the mouse in one hand and my release form in the other. The Stealth bomber's fuel cylinders were safe in my pocket. I felt better than I had since the film crew came to Glenfield, and I really wanted to get home and see my family. I would return what I had taken, get the release form signed, and tell them about my big part in tomorrow's final scene. I wished I knew what it was. But then again, what was a good movie without a little suspense?

Bring in the Stuntman

The next day at the craft fair, I walked around beaming. A city of canvas and tarp covered the park as artists displayed their wares. Rows of booths and tables were filled with handmade objects. There were pots, baskets, glass sculptures, candles, quilts, and even wood carvings. Half the town had turned out, along with visitors from all over.

I squeezed between two elderly ladies to reach Amanda's booth. She greeted me with a wink and a smile.

"Looks great," I said, thankful to see her happy.

She finished with a customer, then turned her attention to me. "Thanks, Willie. I'd show you the mouse, but it was the first thing to sell." She patted her pocket as if to say the price was right.

I gave her a thumbs-up, then ambled toward Dad's booth. He'd been out when I got home the day before, and he had left early this morning. I still needed him to sign the release form. When I got to his booth, though, Mom was the only person in sight.

"Where's Dad?" I asked.

"He forgot something at the store. He'll be back before long," she answered.

The Stealth bomber was on display in the booth. With its black trim and smooth curves, you could practically feel the heat radiating from the wings.

"Any idea what the director wants you to do?"

I shook my head and looked at the ground. Last night I'd told her about my movie break without mentioning the release form.

"Well, you be careful," she warned me. "Don't let the director talk you into something stupid, no matter how convincing he makes it sound."

"I won't," I promised. "I've learned my lesson."

"Good for you," Mom said. "By the way, thanks for returning the Stealth bomber fuel packs so quickly. Today's demonstration means a lot to your father."

"No problem. I shouldn't have taken them in the first place. So when's Dad's first flight?"

"At 11 A.M.," Mom said, glancing at her watch. "One hour and 55 minutes from now."

"It's already after nine?" I gasped, realizing I was late. I considered asking Mom to sign the release form.

Then she repeated herself. "Remember, *Mr. Stuntman*, be careful. Don't let them talk you into something you shouldn't do just because it's a movie."

That settled that. I'd have to come up with another way to get the form signed.

When I arrived at the Pike Estate, the grounds were completely surrounded by people. During the week, spectator interest had dropped off so the crew hadn't needed a barricade to keep the fans out. But today it seemed that everyone not at the craft fair had shown up for a final peek at a movie crew shooting stars right here in Glenfield.

I walked right up to the security guard patrolling along the barricade. Once he heard my name, he quickly let me pass through. That made me feel great. I strutted past carts of technical equipment, fielding greetings from every direction.

"Hey, Plummet," an assistant director called out.

A technician followed suit. "There he is, Mr. Show Business."

"Go get 'em, kid," another added.

I was the man of the hour and loving it. For a moment the attention took my mind off the unsigned release form in my pocket. Then I saw Felix and remembered what I had to do and how he could help me.

"I need a pen," I said, pulling him aside. As a fellow inventor, he always had an assortment of writing tools. He handed me a ballpoint pen, and I quickly signed my dad's name on the release form. I felt guilty doing it, like I had taken the wrong path once again.

But after everything I had gone through to get a part in the movie, I couldn't pass it up.

"What are you doing?" Felix asked, his voice booming with accountability.

"Shhh!" I hissed through clenched teeth. "Why does your voice always change at just the wrong time? You know what I'm doing and it's no big deal. My dad signs release forms for me all the time. He hardly even reads them anymore."

Felix was about to say something when the director ran over and put his arm across my shoulders.

"So how's Mr. Plummet doing today?" he asked. He gave the signed release form to an assistant. "Everything's about ready. Rob told me 15 minutes, max."

"Great. That gives me five minutes to find out what I'm supposed to do and 10 minutes to rehearse. No problem. I can handle it." I laid on the sarcasm a little thick. But with the guilt burning inside me, and so many people watching, I was getting stressed out.

"I know this all seems last minute," the director explained, "But if I didn't think you could handle it, I wouldn't have asked you."

I swallowed hard. "What can I say?"

The director angled me toward the street. "Willie, I haven't forgotten your incredible stunt the other day, when you jumped on the craft services tent to catch Biz. That was amazing. You're an athletic marvel."

"Well, I try to stay in shape."

"It shows. And today it's going to pay off," the director said. "The movie ends with a final battle between Trenton Kyle and the giant raven. If all goes well, it will be one of the most thrilling scenes to come out of Hollywood in a long time."

"Cool," I said, getting excited.

The director beamed. "You want to know what's really cool? We'd like you to be Trenton Kyle's stunt double. We'll give you some platform shoes, stick a wig on your head, and add a few pounds of makeup to your face," the director explained. "When we're done, people will mistake you for the real Hollywood Hunk. What do you say?"

The guilty feeling burned, but I fought it off. "Sign me up. *Stuntman* is my middle name."

"I knew I could count on you," the director said, patting me on the back. He led me to a trailer and told the makeup and wardrobe artists to get busy. They knew just what to do, and after an hour, they had me looking like Trenton Kyle. I wore a sandy brown wig with thick sweaty bangs tossed across my forehead. I had on boots with risers in them, along with jeans and a red flannel shirt. Once the finishing touches were applied, I returned to the front of the barn.

Filming was already under way. Trenton Kyle would be used for the beginning and ending of the final scene. My job was to fill in during the middle, when things got intense. At least that's what the makeup artist thought. The specifics of my task were still a mystery to me.

Easing behind the director's chair, I studied the scene, paying careful attention to Trenton Kyle's mannerisms and position.

"Stay there, Sis, where it's safe," Trenton Kyle warned. He backed away from the barn door. "I couldn't live if something happened to you."

"But I'm scared. We're the only ones left," Sam replied.

"I know. We tried to warn the others, but it's too late. Now I've got to settle this myself."

"Be brave," Sam begged, tears welling in her eyes.

Tears welled in my eyes too, but only because it was so corny.

Trenton clenched his fists. "It's like I said before, Sis. I've got bravery enough for two."

Sam crumbled to her knees, sobbing. With one hand she reached for her brother. With the other she clung to the barn door. An artificial breeze flipped her hair back. Trenton stood his ground, his bronzed face set against the sky.

"Cut!" the director yelled. "Excellent, kids."

Cheering and applause reached us from beyond the barricade.

I watched for reactions from Sam and Trenton. But they didn't budge. Seconds later, I found out why.

"Bring in the stuntman," the director announced.

Rob led me to where Trenton Kyle was standing. An assistant director met us there and helped me assume exactly the same position.

14

Airborne Willie

The director eyed the crowd, then approached me with confidence. "Willie, here's the deal. The mechanical raven has been difficult to work with from day one, leading to revisions in the script. When you took back those special fuel packs, it was yet another curve we had to deal with."

I looked away. "Sorry about that."

"It's all right. We're past that now. In fact, based on what we've come up with, I think we're better for it," the director said. "Here's why—the final battle between Trenton Kyle and the giant raven will occur not on the ground, but in the air."

"In the air?" I asked.

"Exactly," the director confirmed. "Rob replaced your fuel packs with the same kind we use to launch the raven. And he doubled the amount, which means the raven's lifting power will be phenomenal. All you have to do is wait for the raven to swoop down and catch your shoulders. Then you grab its legs, as if you're trying to fight it off. In reality, you're holding on while it lifts you off the ground and over the barn."

The barn loomed over me like a skyscraper, blocking the clouds. "That high, huh?"

"You bet. When you reach the top, just let go and land on the roof," the director said. "We've built a platform up there to make it easier for you. We've also put a camera up there, along with one on top of the house. We'll get every good angle."

"What if the Rocket Raven doesn't lift me that high and we both crash into the front of the barn?" I asked.

"Well, that's a risk we're willing to take," the director answered. "But as long as you start running before the raven catches you, and jump when it does, the odds are in your favor. At least I think they are."

If I wanted to hear the exact opposite of a motivational speech, the director couldn't have done a better job. I tried stalling. "What about the rocket noise? Won't the microphones pick it up?"

"Our sound guys will edit out unwanted noise when the time comes. You leave the technical details to them. My concern is that you know exactly what you're supposed to do and when." The director reviewed my role from start to finish.

"Okay, I think I'm ready," I said, even though I wasn't. Inside me, a tug-of-war was raging between the small gate and the wide one.

As the crew readied themselves, the director returned to his chair.

My mind raced. What if the raven dipped too low and knocked my block off? What if I missed the barn roof and dropped 30 feet? What if …

"Rolling. Background. Action," the director announced.

The Rocket Raven 1000 burst into the sky, leaving a trail of smoke. Rob manned the controls with Felix standing beside him. The sick feeling in my gut spread to every nerve of my body. But it was too late to back down. I turned my attention to the barn. The raven's location was now a mystery. I couldn't see it. I couldn't hear it. I just stared at Sam and nervously twitched my fingers, waiting. The plan was for the raven to take me by surprise. And believe me, it would.

The last thing I noticed before the mechanical raven swooped down was the look of fear on Sam's face. But this time she wasn't acting.

"Ahhh!" I wailed, running for the barn.

The Rocket Raven grabbed my shoulders. Reaching up, I grabbed its legs and jumped on cue.

"*Caw! Caw!*" the raven cried.

The second round of rockets fired, lifting me skyward. I kicked and twisted, as if fighting off the great carnivore. It carried me higher. My feet dangled off the ground, five feet, then ten. The barn loomed in front of us. We struggled to 15 feet. Twenty.

The rockets burned; the wings lifted. But it wasn't enough. The raven carried me straight toward the barn like a human wrecking ball. It couldn't be avoided. I was a goner.

But wait! The door to the loft was cracked open. I could let go and swing through it. The Rocket Raven would soar above the barn and I'd land on a bed of hay. I released my grip and flung my feet forward like battering rams. But the raven held tight! Its claws were caught on my shirt. If I couldn't get loose, we'd crash for sure.

"No!" I shouted, jerking at the claws.

It worked. My shirt came free just in time. The raven flew over the barn just as I crashed through the loft doors and landed in a pile of hay.

"Cut!" the director yelled. Cheers and applause rose to greet me.

The director added his own praise. "Excellent. Nice job, Willie."

Still nervous and in a daze, I climbed down from the loft and headed outside. Everyone met me there.

"Letting go early was a smart call," Rob said. "Otherwise you wouldn't have cleared the roof."

The director nodded. "Next time we'll have to start farther back to get a better run at it. And Rob, you'll need to add a few more rockets."

"Next time?" I questioned. "I don't think so. You saw the claws hook my shirt. I was almost a dead duck."

"I saw it," Sam admitted.

"Willie, you're fine," the director said, putting his arm across my shoulders. "You've got to think like Trenton Kyle for this scene. He's persistent, tenacious. He's up against a mutant raven, and he's not giving up."

"In that case, get him out here," I said.

"I can't risk sending Trenton up there. What if something were to happen to him? That would *really* be terrible. We're depending on you," the director said.

With so much noise coming from the crowd, it was hard to think. The excitement over what would happen next was incredible. The consensus was definitely *go for it*.

But as much as I wanted to please everyone, I kept thinking about the release form I had forged. I had taken the wrong path again, even after everything I had learned. How pathetic. Given the height of the barn and the power of the Rocket Raven, there was no way my dad would have signed the release.

"Well, Plummet?" the director asked.

The tension increased. And so did the noise level of the crew and the spectators. My face burned. I was ready to cave in and just do it.

Then a cracked voice cut through the chaos. It was high-pitched at first, then solid and penetrating. "Willie! Over here!" Felix called out.

Looking around, I found him. He stood at the small gate beside Colonel Pike's house. When my eyes met his, he stepped through. That was all I needed. As much as the stuntman in me wanted to fly, it was the wrong path to follow. I wouldn't make the same mistake again.

"I can't do it," I said. "My dad didn't sign the release. I did."

"What?" the director ranted. He chewed me out, loud enough for everyone to hear. I wanted to bury myself in the ground, but I just stood there and took it.

Apparently Trenton Kyle was listening. He emerged from his trailer and flashed a confident grin. "Take it easy. I'll do the stunt."

The audience burst into applause and cheers. Girls whistled. They were hungry to see Trenton Kyle in action. At first the director protested, but he soon gave in.

"I wouldn't if I were you," I said, walking away.

Trenton ignored my warning and acknowledged the cheering crowd. Moving fast, Rob readied the Rocket Raven 1000 for another flight.

15

That's a Wrap

Trenton Kyle took his position in front of the camera. "You did your best, kid," he told me, "but you're no Trenton Kyle. Let me show you how it's done."

"Ready on props," Rob called out.

Sam moved back to her spot in front of the barn.

"Rolling. Background. Action!" the director said.

In a burst of smoke and light, the Rocket Raven 1000 launched into the air. It climbed into the clouds. When the fuel packs gave out, Rob brought it around. The giant raven swept in a wide turn around the town, then glided back toward the Pike Estate. The rooftop cameras followed it the whole way.

Felix stood next to Rob, giving his input. Since he was the one who'd made the wing adjustments to the Rocket Raven, I think he felt just as nervous as I did.

Trenton held his pose and stared at Sam, waiting.

The raven dipped with a sudden gust, then leveled out. The crowd grew silent.

The Rocket Raven 1000 reached the side of the Pike Estate and zeroed in, ready for contact. It glided in silence, like an eagle swooping down on its prey.

As it neared Trenton Kyle, Rob banked the bird to the right and extended its claws.

"*Caw! Caw!*" the Rocket Raven let out.

Rob eased the giant bird parallel with the ground, then turned it upward. Trenton Kyle took off running. The claws swung down on his shoulders.

"Ahhh!" Trenton grabbed the bird's legs and jumped.

Rob fired the second round of rockets. Liftoff!

The raven angled toward the top of the barn. Rob pulled back on the remote. The wings lifted.

"No!" Trenton Kyle kicked and squirmed.

Talk about playing the part. He acted like he was in a fight for his life. And he was. He and the raven approached the barn. Trenton lifted his feet. Almost there. The raven cleared the roof and kept going.

We watched to see if Trenton would let go, but he didn't. He clung to the bird's legs as if they were parachute cords. As the rockets flared, the bird climbed higher and higher. It zigzagged back and forth like it was ascending switchbacks on a mountain of air. It reached 40 feet in the air, then 50.

I could see Rob frantically adjusting the remote, but the raven didn't respond.

"Do something!" the director shouted.

"The signal's out. The raven isn't responding!"

As people stood there in shock, I took off after Trenton Kyle and the Rocket Raven. Felix followed. I wasn't sure what I would do, but I had to try to help. We sprinted past the barn and down the street. The raven flew higher and higher, cutting back and forth above me. Soon they would reach the hill on the edge of the park where the craft fair was being held.

I had an idea. I checked my watch. Dad's Stealth bomber was scheduled to launch at any moment. I ran ahead, determined to get to Dad in time.

Boom! Schwoosh! The Stealth bomber erupted from the launchpad like a skyrocket. Dad stood on the crest of the hill, watching it go.

I barreled ahead as fast as my feet would take me. Felix kept in stride too.

"Dad!" I screamed, within a hundred yards.

Dad didn't hear me or see the Rocket Raven. His attention was on the Stealth bomber. It finished its rocket-like climb with a sharp U-turn, then headed for the craft fair. At 50 feet from the ground, it leveled off and soared over the tents. Cheers of admiration rose from the exhibitors and shoppers.

"Dad!" I yelled again, but the cheering drowned me out.

"Mr. Plummet!" Felix shouted in a booming voice.

That did it. My dad, along with the rest of the fair, turned to look. He caught sight of the Rocket Raven and the Hollywood Hunk now 70 feet in the air.

"Bring it down!" I screamed.

"What?" Dad called out.

"Bring it down!" Felix thundered.

My dad figured out what was happening. If the Rocket Raven didn't come down soon, it would climb too high to bring Trenton down safely. The wings would function like a hang glider's, but only to a point.

As the Stealth bomber reached the end of the exhibits, my dad pulled back on the throttle and directed it toward the Rocket Raven 1000. He missed it on the first pass. The Rocket Raven soared on, reaching the craft exhibit. Trenton Kyle yelled for help.

My dad lined up the Stealth bomber again, trying to get a lock on his target. He aimed it for the top part of the Rocket Raven's wings.

"That should do it," he said, guiding the Stealth's remote as if he were a fighter pilot.

Crack! Dad was right on target. The Stealth hit the Raven's right wing.

"Yeow!" Trenton screamed as if the raven were picking him up again. But just the opposite was true. Trenton was on his way down. The crash had caused the Rocket Raven to tilt slightly, turning it into a gradual downward spiral directly above the craft fair. It settled to 50 feet. Forty.

Then the jets ran out.

The gradual spiral turned into a sudden swoop. The raven dropped to 20 feet. Ten.

Rip! Trenton and the Rocket Raven 1000 landed on the roof of a canvas tent. As I sprinted down the aisle, I had no idea what was in the booth. Then I thought of Amanda and all the trouble she'd had with her pieces getting broken. Had it really happened again? The shattering of glass answered my question. Amanda's ceramics were safe. Trenton and the Rocket Raven had landed on a tent full of glass sculptures.

When I got there, Trenton was lying facedown on the ground, holding his seat. Seeing the broken glass all around and his cut jeans, I had the feeling he wouldn't be sitting down for a long, long time.

Several people knelt to help Trenton, including one woman who said she was a nurse. Soon the director, Rob, and Sam came running up.

Once the director figured out that Trenton wasn't seriously hurt, he poured on the compliments. "Trenton, you're one of a kind. Absolutely fantastic."

Trenton moaned.

The director got on his walkie-talkie. "Did we get that? How much? All of it? Wonderful, guys. Way to stay with him. Trenton, we got the shot. No more takes today, baby. That's a wrap!"

An ambulance arrived to take Trenton Kyle to the hospital. An assistant director promised the tent's owner that the studio would pay for everything.

That left the director free to talk with us. First, he thanked my dad for helping with his Stealth bomber. Then he turned his attention to me and Felix. "Quick thinking, guys. You really saved Trenton's neck."

"I guess I had the voice for it," Felix joked with falsetto pride.

Finally the director put his hand on my shoulder. "Willie, you made the right call. I can't say I was happy about it at the time, but things worked out."

"I'm just glad I was able to help," I said.

"So am I," the director told me. "And I'd like to show my gratitude with something tangible. We've got some studio work yet to do on the movie, but when it's all done, I'd like to fly you and Felix and Sam to Hollywood for the premiere of *Revenge of the Raven*."

"Awesome," I said. Everyone else agreed.

While Rob and the director talked things over, I confessed to my dad about the release form. He wasn't happy and said we'd discuss it later.

When the director addressed us again, it was to invite us all back to the Pike Estate for a wrap-up celebration. As a crowd gathered around us, we made our way along the street to Colonel Pike's front yard. The security guard moved the barricade for us, but I held back, opting for another route into the backyard. It was the small gate along the side of the house, the one Sam, Felix, and I had first entered to get involved in the movie. I wanted to pass through it again, this time understanding exactly what it meant.

Look for all these
exciting
WiLLiE PLUMMET
misadventures
at your local
Christian
bookstore!